Witchy Wednesday

A Tabitha Chase Days of the Week Mystery

Denise Jaden

Witchy Wednesday

THE MURDER OF A witch, a seaside town selling the supernatural, and a realtor-turned-sleuth rediscovering her purpose.

When self-proclaimed realist and realtor Tabitha Chase takes a trip to small-town Crystal Cove to sell her late aunt's houseboat, nothing is what it seems on the surface, including a local witch's cause of death.

Tabby's spreadsheets and staging skills won't solve the case, but her newly inherited psychic cat might! With the help of a fetching forensics expert and a dashing detective, Tabby hopes to clear her name from suspicion and discover the truth.

Join this witchy cast of characters in the small beach town of Crystal Cove where Tabby may be the only person who can see past the shroud of illusions.

Join my mystery readers' newsletter today!

Sign up now, and you'll get access to a special prequel to accompany this series—an exclusive bonus for newsletter subscribers. In addition, you'll be the first to hear about new releases and sales, and receive special excerpts and behind-the-scenes bonuses.
Visit the link below to sign up and receive your bonus mystery:
https://www.subscribepage.com/witchyprequel

Chapter One

WHEN I WAS A little girl, my Auntie Lizzie told me there were two ways to get to Crystal Cove, Oregon—over the mountains on the interstate or the way she arrived: on a broomstick across the skies.

As an eight-year-old, I'd wanted to believe her stories with everything in me despite the forewarnings of my pragmatic parents. Through the years, and after many real-world obstacles, I'd come to the understanding that those stories were only the fodder of elaborate make-believe, told by people who chose to focus on the imaginary instead of looking head-on at their real-life problems. My learning had become complete a month ago when Aunt Lizzie left a note for her sister, my mom, and then jumped off Crystal Falls to her death.

Crystal Cove used to hold awe and mystique like Disneyland, but as I descended the 101 out of the Calapooya Mountains through rain so slick I could barely see the front of my car, going to take care of some postmortem details, I decided the last tiny part of me that believed in magic had officially died with my aunt.

My windshield wipers squeaked at regular intervals, and my old Honda smelled awful with exhaust, having worked harder than she had in a long time to get up and through the mountain passes. My hands were white-knuckle-locked onto my steering wheel, and I'd been squinting at the road in front of me for almost three hours. This road demanded a lot more than autopilot, but I jumped in my seat when my phone rang through the Bluetooth, letting me know I'd better clue back in.

I fumbled over my phone, not looking away from the road for even a second, and answered, "Hi, Dad. I'm almost there."

The pause that followed made me glance down at my phone screen for one quick heartbeat. Shoot. I'd done it again. It wasn't my dad, who knew all about my trip to Crystal Cove and had pretty much forced it upon me. Nope. It was my boss, Brendan Reiger, who had yet to hear about my impromptu trip and who I had planned to explain it to much more delicately as soon as I had the chance.

"Almost . . . where, Tabitha?" Brendan said through my car's speakers. He had a deep, almost ominous voice. All the realtors in our Portland office thought it was the authority that came with that kind of voice that helped him make so many quick sales. We joked about how his prospective clients were likely scared for their lives if they didn't sign on the dotted line exactly when he told them to. His voice sounded even deeper tonight, which made me momentarily forget my strategic wording and blurt out the truth.

"Oh, yes, well, I just had to take a quick trip down the coast. I, um, I had a death in the family." I hoped he wouldn't ask how recent the death was. I suspected if I had to explain that Aunt Lizzie died almost a month ago, he'd lack the bit of sympathy I had hoped to garner from my tough-as-nails boss.

Instead, he said, "Oh. Who died?"

I blinked hard, trying to split my attention between the rain-soaked road and this phone call. I really should have pulled over—if only I could see the shoulder. "It was my Aunt Lizzie." My voice came out more full of drama than I intended, which only made Brendan pry more.

"Right. Were you close, then?"

I couldn't, in good conscience, say yes. I hadn't seen my aunt in years. But instead I searched for something that might seem like the affirmative. "She was my mom's little sister." Again with the drama, Tabby? Take some acting lessons already!

"And you'll be back tomorrow? We have that showing in Stafford and I hoped I could count on you for putting up signage."

Putting up signage. Was that what my job had become? I'd been giving the Portland real estate market all I had for the past three years. I spent late nights and early mornings drafting market reports, researching amenities, and perfecting my staging skills. At every turn, Brendan suggested I'd be his next superstar realtor, but then he'd saddle me with staging rundown townhouses, blowing up balloons for open houses, and now putting up signage.

"Um, it's a long drive," I said as I passed a weathered wooden sign with faded paint boasting: WELCOME TO CRYSTAL COVE. The road was shrouded with trees on either side, and my GPS showed a few miles yet before I'd reach the town center and then the marina. There were no streetlights out this far, and I continued to squint to see through the rain as I mentally berated myself for picking up the call. "So I probably won't make it back by tomorrow."

"By Tuesday then." It didn't sound like a question. When I didn't say anything right away, he went on. "Our office has been talking to a client from Forest Park. I think they're ready to list, and wouldn't that be the perfect neighborhood for your first solo listing? Wouldn't that make your dad proud?"

My heart rate sped up, both from the idea of my own listing, in Forest Park no less, and from the idea of my father being proud. He was a state senator, and with his endless connections, he'd offered to get me a job with a local realtor as soon as I'd passed the exam, but I'd refused, wanting to prove myself and make my own way in the real estate world. More than once, I'd regretted that quick decision, but now I slowly let a breath seep out of me. Maybe it was time to finally see some fruits from my labor.

I'd barely let out my breath when an obstruction in the middle of the road made me slam on my brakes. I shrieked as the form of a woman came into view. She was lying right in the middle of the rain-soaked road.

"Tabitha?" Brendan asked. "I can count on you to be back on Tuesday, right?"

"I—uh—I have to go." I couldn't tune into Brendan's reply as I slammed my car into PARK, grabbed for my phone, and got out of my car. I left it running, with the windshield wipers working furiously to keep up with the rain and the headlights aimed toward the woman. As I moved closer and pulled the hood of my jacket up over my head, she appeared dead—face up but with one of her jean-clad legs out at an odd angle—spread almost to the splits and bent upward at the knee, which was clearly broken. The odd angles of this woman's body in the midst of the brutal storm with the narrow lighting of my headlights made me momentarily see the situation as a meticulously planned horror movie. I blinked and then shook my head, reminding myself this was real.

"Hello? Hello? Are you okay?" I called. My heart rate ratcheted up as I moved closer and looked into her unblinking eyes. She had striking features—red full lips and thick eyelashes. She looked so alive. My phone was still in my hand, getting soaked, so I tucked it under my jacket and dialed 911.

A second later, a woman answered. "911. What is your emergency?"

"There's a woman. In the middle of the road. I don't think she's breathing."

The operator asked me for my location, and I tried to think as I bent closer to the woman. She wore a bright yellow poncho that looked hand-knit. It immediately made me wonder who had knit it for her—who would be devastated by the news of her passing. "Um. Off highway 101. Just past the welcome sign to Crystal Cove."

I reached for the woman's wrist as the operator confirmed my location. Fresh out of college, I'd attempted a short career as a personal trainer. I'd taken a fitness first aid course, but it felt like a million years ago. Still, training or no training, I knew not finding a pulse was bad news. I explained this to the operator. She instructed me to wait where I was and an emergency vehicle would arrive as soon as possible. After hanging up, I reached for the woman's neck. She was still warm, but I couldn't find a pulse there either. When I pulled my hand away, it was covered in rain mixed with blood.

The metallic scent hit my nose and I gagged. I'd never been great with the sight or smell of blood, and in an instant, I was up and backed against the hood of my car, trying to keep my dinner from three hours ago down in my stomach where it belonged. I kept my eyes from my bloodied hand for long enough that I could catch my breath and hoped the rain would wash the bulk of the blood off before I had to look at it. But the sky chose this moment to close up and stop its torrential downpour.

"Great, the one time I actually want the rain," I murmured toward the sky. My windshield wipers squeaked against the drying glass as I moved back toward my driver's door and found a napkin in the door storage with my left hand while holding my right hand as far as possible away from my nose. I flicked off the wipers, then I held my breath as I wiped off the blood and looked around for somewhere I could dispose of the dirtied napkin.

Never usually one to litter, I couldn't help myself tonight. I tossed it into the roadside bushes. The metallic smell was still playing awful tricks on my stomach. I bent to douse my hand in a nearby puddle as sirens sounded in the distance. My headlights caught something blue and gleaming right beside the puddle.

I picked up what I'd thought was a shiny rock, but it looked more like a tiny jewel once I had it in my hand. I studied the jagged surface. It was smaller than my pinkie nail and probably wasn't worth anything, but it seemed like glass, maybe that sea glass my aunt used to tell me about, and so I tucked it into my jacket pocket and stood as the sirens grew louder and I tried to collect myself.

I walked a wide circle around the woman on the ground, taking note of any details that might be helpful for the ambulance upon its arrival. On her front side, the woman appeared soaked from the rain but otherwise unmarked. Her hair was a strawberry blonde, less red than mine but still red enough to make out the hue even while soaking wet and lit only by my headlights. Now that the rain had subsided, the blood on her neck was visible. Her eyes remained eerily open, looking up at the sky as though she might be waiting to be taken up to heaven.

A firetruck arrived on scene first. It parked at an angle, blocking half the road, and two burly firemen emerged from the front doors.

A third fireman came around from the back of the truck and headed straight for me. "Are you all right? What happened here? Are you injured?"

"No, I'm fine. I didn't hit the woman. She was like this when I arrived." I'd been leaning over to see if I could find anything else of this woman's injuries, but as the fireman moved between me and the woman, I didn't hesitate to take several large steps back.

One of the other firemen quickly set up a large work light, illuminating several feet in all directions of the woman.

"And your name?" the first fireman asked me. He had a square jaw and was clean-shaven, unlike his two coworkers.

"Tabitha . . ." I hesitated, as my father had drilled into me about a thousand times to keep the Chase name as quiet as possible on this trip. But the fireman kept staring at me, a pen poised over his notepad, so I had no choice but to add, "Chase. Tabitha Chase."

Before the fireman could ask me anything more, a dark sedan with blue and red flashing lights and its siren screaming whipped around the corner and parked sideways, blocking the road behind my car. The firetruck blocked most of the road in the other direction, which left all five of us, plus the woman's body, in a small cocoon of space.

A man in a suit, I guessed him to be a detective, emerged from the dark sedan, came around my car, and set his dark eyes squarely on the unshaven fireman. "Tell me what we've got here, Tucker." It sounded more like an order than a question.

"Just arrived on scene, sir."

"Looks like posterior injuries," one of the bearded firemen called out from where he was bent near the woman.

"She's bleeding on the back of her neck," I volunteered helpfully.

The detective's head snapped toward me. "Did you move this woman?"

I shook my head. "No, of course not. I just checked for a pulse."

The detective's brow furrowed, like he wasn't sure he believed me. He also reached to check for a pulse but on her wrist. "Is this the exact placement the woman fell to?" He stood again and loomed over me.

"I—I guess so."

His eyes drilled into me, waiting for more. "Did you move her legs?"

"No! I mean, I just found her like this."

Again with the furrowed brow. "You didn't hit her with your vehicle?"

"No, she was already here," I said again.

"No pulse. Posterior trauma," the clean-shaven fireman said, still making notes. "Mick should be here soon."

The detective nodded and yelled at one of the bearded firemen, who was tilting up the woman's body to have a look at her back. "Are you kidding me, Johnson? Don't move her!" He turned back to the clean-shaven fireman—Tucker—who seemed to be in charge of the firetruck contingent. "She was struck down?" He flipped open his own notebook and started scribbling notes before Tucker had started to answer.

"Well, no, Tom." I found it interesting that the bully of a detective seemed to bark at everyone by their last names, and yet this Fireman Tucker called the detective Tom. "Or I don't know. No pulse, only posterior injuries. But this lady, Tabitha Chase, says she was like this when she arrived." Tucker motioned to me, and the detective turned and set eyes solidly on me for the first time. Or, at least, he set eyes on my brown leather boots. It took about three long seconds for his eyes to travel up the rest of me to my face.

I was an awful mess—soaked through my brown wool coat and even through my sweater. My normally orangey-red hair felt slick against my forehead, and I most certainly didn't feel like being ogled. "Yes, she was like this when I found her," I said for the third time, almost feeling doubt in myself for all the skeptical looks being thrown my way. "It was raining like crazy. I'm just glad I saw her in time to stop and call 911."

"In time?" Tom the detective raised his dark eyebrows at me.

I swallowed, the seriousness of the situation hitting me anew. Because I hadn't seen the woman in time. "I meant in time to stop. So I didn't run over her." My voice dropped, and I bowed my head, belatedly trying to show some respect.

"You got an identity yet?" Tom the detective barked toward the three firemen. He didn't wait for an answer and moved closer to the woman. "Ah.

The Doerksen woman. Another one of those witches."

My head snapped up. "Witches?" I couldn't help but ask. My aunt had told fortunes for a living, so it wasn't as if I was completely unfamiliar with the word. It just seemed so strange, hearing it out of the all-business detective's mouth.

Tom snapped his look back to me. "Do you know this woman?"

I shook my head without looking at her. "I'm not even from here."

"So you've never met Maple May Doerksen?" Tom asked again. Why didn't anyone in this town believe me? It wasn't as though I was the one who'd been a fortune-teller in this town for over twenty years, charging people money to make up stories for them!

"I've never met Maple May Doerksen," I said, deadpan.

Before Tom the detective could question me further, a light-colored sedan arrived. It parked in the small gap of road left unoccupied by the firetruck and the detective's sedan, and that's when I noticed the lineup of lights down the road in the darkness. Traffic, it seemed, had accumulated, but unlike in the city where people would be honking their horns by now, people had gotten out of their vehicles and stood in a group at a distance, whispering about the scene in front of them.

The man in the light sedan was the "Mick" they had been waiting for. Mick wore a white lab coat and studied the body on the road while the detective stood nearby, updating him with everything he'd heard from me and Fireman Tucker.

It seemed as though everyone had forgotten about me. When I shivered again from the cold seeping through to my skin, I sidled up beside the bearded fireman who had returned to his truck. "Excuse me? Do you think it's all right if I go now?"

He took one glance over my shoulder at my car. "Don't think you'd be able to, even if it was okay."

I turned and saw what he meant. Not only was my car blocked by the detective's sedan, but now there were a half dozen vehicles lined up behind that.

I nodded my thanks and headed back to my car. The engine was still running, burning a lot of gas, and my headlights were still on. I got into my driver's seat, turned off my headlights, and cranked up my heat. The firemen had set up three portable lights by this time, so I didn't think the absence of my headlights would make any difference, but the moment they flicked off, Tom's gaze snapped to my car and he marched straight over.

I unrolled my window as he said, "Where do you think you're going?"

I clearly wasn't going anywhere, but his tone made me angry. "I'm warming up! I'm soaked right through all my clothes, and you gave me no idea how long I might be here, so I had no choice but to take care of myself."

Tom the detective nodded. "Take care of yourself." Again, his words made me feel like I was responsible for this horrible accident. He didn't stay to accuse me of anything outright, though.

Instead, he strode to the front of my car, squatted, and started studying it with a flashlight.

This guy was too much.

Cold or not, I buttoned up my coat and got out of my car. I stomped around to the front. "Look, I told you I didn't hit that lady with my car. I've told you and your firemen three times, and I have no idea why you keep—"

He stood and got right in my face. "Well, if you didn't run into Maple May, why is there blood on your hood? Would you like to tell me that?" He shone the flashlight at my light blue Honda Civic, and sure enough, there was a streak of dark red across the front edge of the hood. "I'll bet you a million dollars if we test it, it'll match up with Maple May's blood."

My mind scrambled for an answer as I burned with anger. Had I hit the woman and knocked my head and forgotten the whole thing? Was I completely delusional? But then my answer burst out of my mouth the second it came to me. "That was from me! My hand." Tom tried to interrupt, but I didn't let him. "I'd tried to take the woman's pulse . . . while I was on the line with 911. My hand got blood on it, and I wiped it—"

"You wiped it on your car?" He raised an unbelieving eyebrow at me.

I waved toward the bushes. "No, Tom." If he was going to talk to me like I was stupid, I was determined to do the same right back to him. "I wiped it on a napkin, but I guess I got some on my car. Yes, it will match that woman's blood, but no, I absolutely did not hit her with my car!"

Tom took his flashlight toward the bushes. When he located the offending napkin, he pulled out a small plastic Ziploc with the word "Evidence" emblazoned on the side. I resisted the urge to roll my eyes. After all, if these people still chose to believe I had hit the woman with my car, I didn't have a lot of ways to prove otherwise.

After that, Tom took a swab of "evidence" from the front hood of my car. He turned to me when he was done. "I'll need your driver's license and registration, please, ma'am." I bent into my car to retrieve them but not before he spoke his next words to me. "And I'd also love an explanation for why you think it's appropriate to call me Tom."

Chapter Two

I STARED AT THE detective for a long moment with my driver's license in one hand and my insurance papers in the other. Sure, I was angry, but getting on this detective's bad side before I'd even made it into Crystal Cove seemed like the last thing I should do.

"I didn't mean to be disrespectful. I just heard Mr. Tucker over there call you Tom."

The detective cleared his throat. "It's Detective Thom. T-H-O-M." Before I had a chance to respond, he snatched my license and papers from my hands and, without another word, strode purposefully back to his car with them.

What a jerk! I was in no hurry to talk to Detective Thom again, but he returned what seemed like seconds later.

"Where were you planning on going from here, Miss Chase? I see you live in Portland."

I nodded once. "I'm headed into Crystal Cove for a short time. A day or two at most."

The detective studied my face for a long moment before he spoke. "I'll need a phone number and address for where you'll be staying here in town."

I gave him my cell number and the address for the marina where my aunt's houseboat was docked. I wasn't sure if Aunt Lizzie's boat was going to be the most comfortable place for me to stay. I hadn't slept on her couch since I was eight, but I figured I could always find a nearby hotel tomorrow.

"Which boat?" Detective Thom asked.

"I—uh—" Suddenly, I was certain he'd know exactly who my Aunt Lizzie had been, and that was the last thing I needed at the scene of the death of a local witch. But it seemed I had no choice. "Um . . . the Lady of Fortune?" I asked it as a question, even though I'd known the silly name for my aunt's boat since I could talk.

The detective looked back at my license before handing it back over. "The Lady of Fortune?" His tone seemed too light for the moment or this information. "And can you tell me who you plan to visit there?"

He was playing with me, trying to trap me. I could feel it. My dad had told me to keep quiet in town about my relationship with Aunt Lizzie. The last thing he needed for his campaign was a connection to a recent suicide. But this was different. This was the police, and I clearly needed to come clean with the whole truth if I was ever going to get out from under Detective Thom's suspicion.

"Lizzie Rose was my aunt," I told him. "I'm here to clean up her houseboat and get it up for sale. That's all."

His eyes moved side to side over mine for a few seconds, as if he were trying to read any lies. I kept mine squarely locked on his.

But before he could respond, Mick in the white lab coat called him over. "Hey, Thom. Come and look at this."

I waited and watched while they had a quiet conversation over the dead woman's body. I'd never seen a dead person in real life, and the more I looked at Maple May Doerksen, the more it seemed unbelievable that she wouldn't simply sit up and start talking again. How could she truly be dead? And so instantly? I looked again around the scene, now blocked in by emergency vehicles and lit like a movie set.

I couldn't hear much of what Detective Thom or the medical examiner were saying, but when the detective left the man in white, he told him, "I'll likely have to get Jameson in on this one." Then he returned to me and instructed me to wait in my car until he had a chance to clear the traffic and make a path for me to get out. He passed me a business card. "And I'd appreciate it if you'd let me know before you leave town, in case we have any further questions."

I took his card, agreed, and got back into my now-cold vehicle. Even once I had it idling and pumping out the heat full blast, I couldn't seem to warm up.

I'd seen a dead body tonight.

I'd almost run her over.

And worst of all, Detective Thom had accused me of killing her.

If I believed in bad omens, that would most definitely be what the start of this trip felt like.

Chapter Three

IT WAS AFTER MIDNIGHT by the time I found the Crystal Beach Marina. It wasn't very well lit, and I didn't have much in the way of memories of which boat was my aunt's. Had I known I would arrive this late, I definitely would have booked a hotel.

I sighed and got out of my car, thankful that the rain was continuing to hold off for the moment. I'd brought a small wheeling suitcase with my overnight things, and it clacked and bumped over the wooden slats of the wharf as I followed my mom's written directions to where I'd find the Lady of

Fortune. I had no idea if others lived on boats here and if I might be clacking by anyone's beds, but I was too exhausted to care enough to pick up my suitcase.

I passed a few small sailboats that didn't look large enough to have inhabitants and then made a left toward the bigger boats. When the first fancy yacht came into view, I couldn't help myself and hoisted my suitcase up by its handle with a grunt. Everything seemed silent, aside from the waves lapping at the sides of the wharf. There were only three large motorized yachts in a line before I came to the houseboats.

As a child, I'd had a romanticized view of living on a houseboat, but as I passed each of the dilapidated structures now, trying to recognize my aunt's, my realtor's brain kicked in, and even in the dark, I noticed water abrasions and could immediately name a dozen bits that needed sprucing up.

But if I thought the bits and pieces of wear on the first couple of houseboats were bad, that was nothing compared to when I finally came to the boat labeled "ady of F tune" in the final slip on this wharf.

A wash of memories overtook me as I stared up at the multi-colored flags strung from mast to tip, the purple curtains flounced under the second-story overhang, and the wrought iron furniture on the front deck. When I was an eight-year-old, this boat had felt like an attraction at a theme park, but now that I was as an adult, and even in the dark, the large structure didn't look like something I wanted to climb aboard. The rusty old vessel looked like more of a sailboat or even a tugboat than a boxy houseboat. The other ones in the line seemed more like real houses—part of the real estate market—simply balancing on the water, but my aunt's boat looked as though it had once been sea-worthy—though I would not trust it outside of the harbor now.

I looked again to the wrought iron table and chairs, now rusty, and purple bejeweled drapes, trying to remember if that was where my aunt had done her fortune-telling.

The rear of the boat had two stories of interior space, but the only door to get inside was via the front deck. I held a rail on the boat as I stepped across the short gangplank that joined it to the wharf and immediately felt my legs wobble from the transition. Once fully aboard the boat, I took a couple of seconds to let my body adjust to the regular movement from the waves. Then I headed for the door and rustled the key my mom had given me out by the time I made my way under the purple curtains.

At first, the key didn't turn at all. In a panic, I jiggled it and pushed the door with my shoulder at the same time, and thankfully it started to give way. With a little more force, it eventually nudged open. Silence greeted me. It didn't feel like the safest place to stay by myself at night. In fact, it seemed as though there was no one else around the entire marina.

But the idea of leaving and finding a hotel tonight exhausted me, and even the thought brought my eyes to half-mast.

"I'll fix the doorknob first thing tomorrow," I murmured to myself, pushing the rest of the way through the door and then using my phone's flashlight to look around a bigger space than I remembered.

I'd visited my aunt a handful of times when I was little, usually for long weekends when my parents took an adults-only vacation to Wine Country, California. My brother and sister always chose to stay back in Portland with friends, but my first choice had always been Aunt Lizzie's. The last time I'd been here, I'd gone home with stories of magic spells and spiritual eyesight, and my parents had decided she wasn't a great influence on me. After that, my mom started to visit her half-sister a few times a year on her own, and my parents hired a sitter to stay with us in Portland when they went away.

The interior of the boat brought more memories: the sea air, mixed with a hint of mildew. That ever-present motion that made you feel a mix of unsteady and peacefully rocked. The homey warm orange colors decorating the loveseat and chairs and even some braided artwork on the walls. My dad had spoken of the boat as a commodity so many times in the last month that I'd momentarily formed a clinical picture in my head. Now my aunt's spiritedness came flooding back in every inch of what had been her home.

This was also fortune-telling-central. That was clear by the wooden table with a chair on either side, flouncing purple-and-orange tablecloth with beaded tassels, and a crystal ball on a thick wooden base, right at the center of the table.

I'd yet to find a light switch in this boat, and when my phone light went dim and a second later something rubbed up against my chins, I nearly came out of my skin.

I shrieked and jumped away in one motion. Fumbling over my phone, I eventually got the lights turned back on in time to see what I initially thought was a small raccoon that had followed me onto the boat. But after only a second of my eyes adjusting, I saw instead a cat with legs so short, its belly hung almost to the floor.

"Shoo! Shoo!" I told it, waving my free hand. My parents had never had any pets—Mom was physically allergic, while Dad was emotionally allergic—and so I didn't have a high comfort level around cats, dogs, hamsters, or even fish. What I knew about stray cats came from TV and included sharp claws, urine spraying, and rabies.

But the squat gray striped cat didn't listen and instead skirted right between my legs and deeper into the boat.

"Hey, come back here!" My voice gave away my utter exhaustion, and when I shone my flashlight around the entire space and couldn't locate the cat, I decided that would just be one more thing I had to put out of my mind if I was going to get any sleep at all tonight. There was so much work to be done on this boat before selling it—what would be the difference if I had to clean up a little cat pee?

At least in the process of trying to find the cat, I located the door to the upper deck and my aunt's bedroom.

I figured I'd had enough bad fortune for one day. The universe must be able to see that.

Chapter Four

MY AUNT'S BED HAD a luxurious queen-size mattress. Even with all the fears and questions rattling around my head, I slept until almost eleven the next morning, when I woke in the midst of a dream. I was by the roadside again, near the WELCOME TO CRYSTAL COVE sign, but this time my boss, Brendan, and three other top realtors from his office walked around the dead woman's body, surveying it, and then adding blue throw pillows around her as if decorating or staging the scene. I shook my head at the strange dream and was shocked when I turned on my phone and saw I already had five missed calls, all from my dad.

This quickly woke me up and brought me back to reality. Dad rarely had time to call people back once, let alone five times.

"I wanted to make sure you got that house on the market first thing," he said by way of a hello.

I resisted the urge to yawn and blinked away the sleep from my eyes. "Well, it's not exactly a house, Dad."

After seeing it, I had to wonder if I could even list it through the regular real estate channels. I didn't know. Maybe I'd have more luck selling it through the boat trader website or even Facebook Marketplace.

"So you still haven't listed it?" Dad used his fake-pleasant voice, which meant there must have been someone else in his office.

"Dad, just give me a break here. You wouldn't believe what happened to me on my way into town last night. I almost drove over a dead body on the road, and I'm pretty sure the police wanted to arrest me for it—" I couldn't get another word out. If I'd been more awake, I would have watched my phrasing a little closer.

"What!" He dropped his voice to a panicked whisper. "Was it a human body? Tell me the papers haven't gotten a hold of this, Tabitha." Then louder, "Mary, we need to do some damage control down in Crystal Cove."

Mary had been Dad's secretary since he was first voted into office three years ago. They made an efficient team, almost always cleaning up any public gossip about the family before it hit the media.

"No. It's fine. I wasn't arrested. They just held me there for a good part of the night until it was clear I hadn't hit the woman with my car. But it was late by the time I got here and the boat is in awful shape. It'll need an overhaul before I can list it."

"I'm counting on you to take care of that as soon as possible. And remember, keep the Chase name out of it—you're just the realtor." I'd already been forewarned about this part. Dad had been determined to keep his association with Lizzie Rose out of the news. That was why Dad only trusted me to take care of this as quickly and quietly as possible, so it didn't affect his current campaign.

"I'd love to, but I don't know any tradespeople down here, and Brendan was already calling me last night, eager for me to get back to Portland." Remembering my strange dream from last night was helping me not to think of my job situation with Brendan too seriously. "Apparently, there's a listing in Forest Park coming up and he wants me back so I can take the lead on it."

Dad scoffed. "Get your head out of the clouds, Tabitha. Brendan is never going to offer you a listing in Forest Park. Why wouldn't he give those properties to his best agents?"

Why, I wanted to say, is because he sees potential in me. Because, unlike my father, Brendan Reiger thought I could make something of myself.

"He's promised this sort of thing before," Dad went on. "And has he followed through, even once?" Thankfully, Dad didn't leave time for me to answer before changing the subject again. "Besides, your mother really needs you to do this, Tabby." He only called me Tabby these days when trying to play the director role in my life. It was his way of reminding me that inside I was still the little incapable little girl I'd always been. "Hasn't she been through enough?"

The rhetorical questions were too much. "I'll see what I can do." Before I could say anything else, a loud mrreoooww reminded me of another problem. "Hey, do you know if Aunt Lizzie had a cat?"

She'd died almost a month ago, so I figured it was more likely a stray. But then Dad said, "Is that thing still hanging around? Your crazy aunt spent seven hundred dollars on a pair of eyeglasses for that cat. What kind of a cat needs glasses?"

As Dad asked yet another rhetorical question, my mind returned to the night before. There had been something unusual about the cat, but my tired brain had written it off until this second. That was what it was. The cat I'd seen last night had been wearing eyeglasses, hadn't it?

Another mreowww sounded, and so I said, "Listen, Dad, I've got to go, but I'll give you an update as soon as I can." With that, I hung up.

The cat waited right on the other side of the door to the lower deck, looking up at me through his spectacles. They were held on his head by an elastic strap, which he seemed unbothered by. Now that I was wide awake, I had to admit, the glasses added a certain amount of character.

"What do you want? Food?" I guessed. "Or do you need to go out for the bathroom?"

I pushed past the cat onto the lower floor, and he padded behind me as I made my way to the outside door. After getting the fiddly lock open, though, I held the door, and the cat just sat on his haunches and stared up at me.

"No bathroom, huh?" I murmured. "I hope that doesn't mean you already went somewhere."

I moved back into the center of the room and then turned in a circle, surveying the place. A small kitchen sat off to the rear of the boat. Then there was the sitting area with the small loveseat and the table with the crystal ball. A bureau sat off to the other side, the top covered with bottles of what looked like perfumes or, more likely, potions. The bureau had a dozen drawers along the front, many of them bulging open with papers or colorful scarves. On an upper shelf sat a dozen books that looked like they were all those true-crime types of detective novels.

I certainly had my work cut out for me. I wondered if anything around here could be sold separately for any amount of money or if I should just have the nearest thrift store come and take what they wanted. The real estate market in

Oregon had taken a dive in the past year, which was another reason it might be better to post it in the boating markets. Except for the fact that I had no idea how to go about doing that.

The cat meowed again and so I headed for the kitchen. "Lizzie must have kept some food for you around here somewhere, right?" I asked the cat and then immediately wanted to smack myself for talking to something that clearly couldn't answer me back.

But then the cat stepped up beside me, hopped onto his hind paws, and perched up at the top of a lower cupboard with his front ones. A second later, he had it pulled open.

Not only that, but I watched in awe as he knocked over a tall plastic container less than half full of kibble. Then he placed one paw on top of the container and used the other to pry off the lid. From there, he stuck his head right inside the mouth of the container and proceeded to have his breakfast.

While he ate, I shook my head, stunned at his competence. It took me several long minutes to shake it off, and then I opened all the upper cupboards in the small kitchen, which were filled with canned goods and dried pasta and enough dishes only for one.

When I looked back, the cat had—I kid you not—replaced the lid on his food container and somehow tilted it back upright. I opened my mouth to say something, even just to myself, but then the cat moved over and started pawing at another lower kitchen cupboard. By the time I got there, he had lifted onto his hind legs and had the door wide open.

"That's quite the skill." I chuckled. "But I don't think your owner would have wanted you going through all of her cupboards." As I said this, I wondered about cats and how much they understood about loss. Did this cat even notice his owner was gone? Or had he only noticed the lack of fresh food?

Then again, he'd been locked out for nearly a month. He must have scavenged food from somewhere.

He pawed at something inside the cupboard. I squatted to look at what had him so interested. A coffee can. "Did Lizzie keep food in here for you, too?" I picked up the can, but it felt empty. I pried the lid open, and sure enough, there were barely any grounds left inside and definitely no cat food. However, the scent that hit my nose quickly reminded me I hadn't had my morning coffee yet. No wonder I wasn't thinking clearly.

"Wow, you're a pretty smart cat. You seem to know what we both need."

But Lizzie was out of coffee, and looking around, I didn't even see a coffee maker.

"I don't suppose you know where to find the nearest coffee shop?" I asked the cat and then wanted to swat myself again.

But this cat, this short, spectacled, intelligent-looking cat, padded over to the bureau, placed his paws on the highest drawer he could reach, and then proceeded to paw at the air above him.

I tilted my head and looked at the art hung on the wall above the bureau. It appeared to be a map, all hand-drawn in pastels with cartoonish landmarks. Moving closer, I could see the hand-drawn words "Crystal Cove" along the bottom. The marina was drawn with a few sailboats off to the left, and I followed the road from it with my finger until it reached Main Street. My finger stopped on a large hand-drawn coffee cup.

I looked sidelong at the cat, not allowing myself to believe this feline could understand me.

Nevertheless, I opened my mouth to say, "Careful, kitty. If you keep giving me this kind of help, I just might want to take you home."

Chapter Five

THE CAT DIDN'T WANT to leave the boat while I headed out for coffee, but I figured I'd gotten lucky without him peeing inside so far, so I picked him up, held him at a distance, and placed him on the wharf beside my aunt's boat.

He tilted his head up at me and blinked a few times fast. If I could have recognized confusion in an animal's face, I would have sworn that was what he showed on his. I said, "I won't be long," finally giving in to the fact that I was probably going to keep talking out loud to that cat if he kept hanging around.

I'd taken a snapshot of my aunt's artsy map with my phone, wondering if she had drawn the piece herself or if it might have been drawn by a local artist. Because the café looked close enough to walk, I grabbed my umbrella from my car in case the rain started up and headed that way on foot.

The trek was a little longer than expected, but the cool spring air did something to clear my head. As I made my way up from the water toward Main Street, I let out a melancholy sigh. I'd grown up in Portland, and while I knew I'd want for amenities in a small town like this one, I'd always felt a little like a nameless faceless person in the bustle of the big city. Memories of staying here with Lizzie included walking through town with her and having my aunt greet everyone we passed by name. I'd daydreamed about the charm of small towns, where people knew you and you felt important or at least useful. If only I'd come and spent more time with my aunt while she was alive.

My parents thought they knew best about where to bring me up, what college I should attend, and even whether or not I should ever own a pet. I'd thought I was being independent a few years ago when I'd finally moved out of their large house and into my very own tiny apartment, but it wasn't until this moment, walking toward the downtown core of a tiny quaint town, that I realized how many ideas I'd shut myself off from, simply because I was my parents' daughter.

The pace felt slow as cars passed me, like they didn't have anywhere in particular to be. I passed a tire shop where a mechanic leaning under a car's hood in its one bay stood upright and waved at me as I went by. I did a double take to make sure there wasn't someone behind me that he actually knew, but I didn't see anyone.

I smiled a hesitant smile and waved back.

I passed a hairstylist, a bookstore, and two metaphysical gift shops. I was surprised a town this size would support more than one. But something I remembered of my Aunt Lizzie from when I visited as a child was her telling me again and again that this—Crystal Cove—was where the magic happened.

I had been eager to believe in magic back then, and even the name Crystal Cove sounded magical. Eventually, my belief in magic had been replaced by the understanding that wanting something to be true doesn't make it so, and now I found my feet firmly planted in a land called Realism.

Still, the feeling of the small town, along with its unique shops and memories, brought back a certain nostalgia.

At long last, I came upon The Heirloom Café. By this time, my mouth was watering for a cup of coffee, and I glanced over a handwritten chalk sandwich board that boasted their specials on the sidewalk out front.

I was normally a regular two cream and sugar kinda girl, but my eyes lingered on the lavender latte, and I wondered what it would taste like. I heard my dad's voice in my head: go with the safe bet, Tabitha. Experimenting never got me anywhere.

Well, maybe it had never gotten him anywhere, but going with the safe bet wasn't my campaign slogan. Being in this town, this place that seemed so far removed from my normal life, made me want to try new things—even if just an exotic cup of coffee.

The bell jangled as I pushed through the glass door. It was a large place, with tables of seating on two split levels. A few women sat on the upper level near the rear of the café, hunched together in quiet conversation. Several round tables were strewn throughout the open space with purple and green and yellow beaded jewelry on top, as well as handmade cards. It looked like this café also doubled as a metaphysical gift store.

A twentysomething male barista with dark hair and long sideburns that gave him a 1960s vibe stood behind the counter. He greeted me with a wide smile.

"What can I get for you?" His name tag read AVRUM.

"I'd love to try your lavender latte." I pointed to a glass case between us. "And maybe a basil and chive muffin?"

"Coming right up." He bent to grab my muffin. "You here from out of town?"

"It's that obvious?"

He chuckled lightly. "I know all the regulars, but we get a lot of tourists, too."

It made sense, then, why the town could support so many gift shops.

"Your latte'll be a couple minutes. While you're waiting, feel free to browse the sales items or the bulletin board, if you're looking for something to do while you're in town."

I opened my mouth to tell him I was most definitely not looking for more to do while I was in Crystal Cove. But then I stopped myself because opening that conversation would inevitably leave me having to glaze over my identity and the true purpose for my visit.

Instead, I smiled my thanks and wandered past a couple of tables of beaded dream catchers and long necklaces before turning for the large message board that took up a good ten feet of wall space. The cork-style board had papers tacked over every square inch—advertisements for harp lessons and tarot card readings and Saturday spiritual socials. More advertisements held rental spaces and cars for sale. I wondered briefly if a sale flyer for my aunt's boat would garner any notice if I posted one in here. Most of these flyers were either handwritten or on basic white photocopy paper with plain text. If I made up a color flyer with a few well-taken photos of the boat, it might grab some interest, especially if this place brought in a lot of tourists—perhaps tourists with extra spending money.

But that would entail fixing it up, at least enough so it would show well. I still hadn't gotten my head around how much work that would be.

My eyes drifted to a poster in the middle of the board.

Join us for Witchy Wednesdays
Right here at The Heirloom Café

7 p.m. All are welcome!

Witchy—did that mean there were real witches in attendance? Was it some kind of coven? It said all were welcome, so I didn't suppose it was an exclusive coven, at the very least. I tried to remember what Mom had told me about Aunt Lizzie's so-called witchcraft. It wasn't like the witchcraft some acquaintances back in Portland practiced, I knew that much. More like what came to mind with fairy-tale witches, only on the side of good. I couldn't recall more than that, though.

I wondered if the witch I'd found dead on the road last night had ever come to Witchy Wednesday. I wondered if my aunt had ever attended a group like that one.

Again, I felt a pang of regret that I'd so easily obeyed my parents for all those years, even after I was out of their house. I wished I'd come to see Aunt Lizzie, at least one time that I'd be able to clearly remember.

"Your lavender latte's ready," Avrum called.

When I went to get it from him, I realized I hadn't specified that I'd like it to go. As he passed me a large mustard-yellow mug that perfectly complemented the purple lavender sprinkled beautifully over a swirl of foam, I decided I couldn't ask him to transfer cups. Not when it looked so pretty.

"That lavender looks so . . . fresh." I wasn't sure if that was the right word, as it was clearly in dried form, but I guess I'd expected some sort of shaker cup of store-bought lavender flavor mixed in.

"Yep. I grind all the herbs and spices right here with our pestle and mortar." He motioned to a large stone bowl on the rear counter. The pestle that went with it must've been massive, though I couldn't spot it to be sure. I glanced at Avrum's meaty forearms poking out from his white short-sleeve button-down shirt, and they suddenly made a lot of sense on his wiry frame. I'd seen a pestle and mortar used once on a cooking show. I remembered wondering what kind of person had that kind of time to invest in the ingredients, let alone the cooking. Now I knew.

But at the same time, I had to admit, I was excited to try the latte and muffin now that I knew just how much work had gone into them.

"It looks amazing." I dropped two dollars into the glass tip jar on the counter. "Thank you."

I took a seat near the counter, not wanting to disturb the ladies in the rear of the café, as they appeared deep in conversation. As I surveyed two of them in long flowing skirts and another in a black minidress paired with black-and-white striped tights, I wondered if they could be witches. I didn't know if witches came with a dress code, and the lady I'd found in the middle of the road last night in jeans and a knit poncho had certainly not looked like what I would have expected from a witch.

"What are the Witchy Wednesday meetings like?" I asked Avrum the moment it came to mind.

He was now busy kneading dough on the counter. "Oh, you should definitely check it out. Hard to describe—filled with colorful people, but no meeting ever seems the same."

I had to admit, it sounded intriguing. But I most certainly would not be here until Wednesday. I glanced toward the rear of the café again, wondering if those ladies were indeed witches and if they'd already heard about the lady, Maple May something-or-other, who had died on the road last night.

As if Avrum could read my thoughts, he told me, "That's Marigold Weathers back there. If you have more questions about Witchy Wednesday, you should ask her."

His voice was loud, and the woman in the bright red skirt with matching lipstick turned our way. "Ask me what, dear?"

Marigold Weathers had to be at least sixty, but her hair was dyed a bright purple in a way that it would have more suited someone half her age. She was stocky for a woman—not fat, but strong-looking. Without the long skirt and the purple hair, I might have mistaken her for a man.

"Oh. Um. Avrum here was telling me that you would know about Witchy Wednesdays, but I don't think I'll be in town—"

"Of course!" she said, coming toward me with wide-open arms like she might be about to give me a hug.

I wasn't much of a touchy-feely person, so I backed right against my chair.

But instead, when she got close, she clapped her hands together loudly. "Now, do you have some powers yourself or are you simply an interested observer?"

"An interested observer?" I nibbled my lip, wondering how I'd gotten myself into this conversation.

"Well, bring your coffee and muffin and come up here and sit! We'll tell you all about it!"

As it turned out, the four ladies in the upper section of the café were all a part of Witchy Wednesdays.

"Now come on, ladies. Gather round," Marigold told them. "We need to fill our new friend in on our Witchy

Wednesdays. She's an interested observer." Marigold Weathers nodded with arched eyebrows as if this phrasing meant something very specific, and in fact, when I looked around, all four women nodded with understanding. "This is Rachael Adams." Marigold motioned to the young woman of about twenty, who wore the black-and-white striped tights I'd seen from across the room. Rachael, of any of them, looked the part of the typical witch. Despite her obvious endeavor to have a striking witchy fashion sense, though, her brown mousy brown hair fell at her shoulders as though it hadn't even been brushed today.

Marigold motioned to the other long-skirted woman. "This is Ruth—just Ruth—and she's our local potions specialist." Ruth was in her thirties and wore much more muted colors—a brown skirt with a gray coat.

As Marigold introduced the fourth member of the group, I quickly forgot about Ruth. "This is Donna Davine. She's an expert in spells. Now sit, sit! Ask us all your questions!"

Donna wore jeans and a fitted turtleneck. She was mid-twenties, the closest in age to me, but she reminded me most of the witch who had died on the road last night, although with much sharper features. Her slanted eyebrows gave her an appearance of being angry, even when she smiled.

Marigold pulled up an extra chair for me. I didn't know if it was a matter of my tired brain and all the overwhelming details of the houseboat or just being in Crystal Cove, but I had the sudden feeling like I wanted to stay here with these ladies all day. In a matter of only five minutes, they had made me feel like I belonged with them—and I wasn't even a witch!

I sat and then nibbled at a bite of my muffin to stall. What questions did I have? But I'd barely asked myself that internal question when some queries came to me. "You mentioned Ruth specialized in potions and Donna with the spells." Marigold looked down and pursed her lips at this. "Does everyone here have their own specialty?" I wondered if Aunt Lizzie was the only fortune-teller in town or if there were others. But of course I couldn't ask that outright without them wondering how I had known Lizzie.

"Some of us do," Ruth explained. She motioned to Marigold. "And some of us have more than one gift."

At this, Marigold looked up at me and beamed. "What was your name, dear?"

"Tabby—Tabitha," I told them. I'd been slowly getting more comfortable in introducing myself to real estate clients as Tabitha, as both my father and Brendan assured me it sounded more professional than Tabby, but once in a group of women like this, I quickly felt the urge to revert back to Tabby. I reminded myself of my true purpose for being here—to sell something that I still couldn't decide if it was or was not classified as an actual house.

"Ahh, Tabitha. I've always loved that name." Marigold reached across the table and took my hand, which was just about to reach for my lavender latte. I wondered if one of her many gifts was palm reading and if she was attempting to discover something about me right this second. I leaned forward a little in curiosity. But then I reminded myself I didn't believe in all that. "And tell us . . . how did you hear about Crystal Cove?"

I had to choose my words carefully. "I came into town on business. I drove in late last night to look at a houseboat I'm supposed to be selling for the owner."

Marigold and Ruth, the long-skirted two of the group, looked at each other. "Late last night? What time did you get in?" Marigold seemed to do most of the speaking in the group.

I wondered if their concern stemmed from the fact that their friend had been killed on the road. "Actually, I planned to get her by ten, but there was a horrific accident on my way into town." I didn't really want to be the one to break the news to them if they hadn't heard it, but at the same time, I could only front so many half-truths before they'd see through me.

With this thought, I decided to pull my hand away and avoid Marigold's eyes as much as possible.

But then they all looked down at the table at my words, confirming that this was not news.

Marigold was the first to look up. "You saw it then? The accident on Polaris Road?"

I nodded solemnly. "I was actually the first to arrive on scene and call 911." If this was their friend, I'd tell them everything they wanted to know. When my dad had informed me that Aunt Lizzie had jumped from the cliff to her death, even though I was estranged from her for many years, I'd asked a lot of questions, enough until it felt real and the weight of it really sank in. Dad had answered them all as plainly and unemotionally as possible, and I would do the same for these ladies.

"You just drove up and found her there?" Rachael asked. Worry lines etched her forehead and tears formed in her eyes.

I nodded. "It was raining so hard that I almost didn't see her. I had to slam on my brakes and then I hopped out of my car with my phone right away to see if she was still breathing."

"Raining?" Rachael looked at the others with serious eyes. "So it would have washed away any evidence."

My forehead furrowed. These four had clearly heard about the accident, and it sounded as though the police hadn't discovered who had caused the hit-and-run yet. In hopes of letting them know not all of the evidence had been washed away, I told them, "Actually, the medical examiner was still able to see a lot of the trauma along her backside, and it stopped raining soon after I arrived, so the police may be able to figure it out yet." I'd watched enough CSI episodes to know that hit-and-run accidents often left dents of evidence as well as traces of blood and hair that the naked eye might not see. I decided not to mention that my car had been suspicious for a short time. These ladies didn't need to hear that.

"So you saw her?" Rachael asked me, her face contorted in pain. I got the feeling she was the closest of the four to Maple May. "How did she look?"

"On the front, she looked fine, actually. Well, other than her strangely bent leg." I still couldn't quite get my head around how getting knocked down with a vehicle would have forced her leg into such an odd angle.

"Bent leg? How was she lying?" Rachael asked.

"On her back, curved with her arms at her sides. One of her legs was stuck out at an odd angle. That's what made me realize right away that something was wrong with her."

"Odd angle how?" Rachael pressed. It almost sounded like a note of anger in her voice.

"Like a . . . ?" I held out my hands, trying to come up with the word for the hiking tool I was thinking of. "I've used one rock climbing before." I looked around, wondering how I could best describe it, as I didn't particularly want to get down on the floor to show them.

There was a metal napkin dispenser on the table. I got an idea and pulled out a few napkins. After laying one flat to indicate Maple May's body, I ripped a couple in half and rolled them up to indicate her limbs. The arms were easy to place, but when I finally got the legs into the position I'd seen the night before, gasps sounded from all around the table.

"It looks just like your Destiny Goddess Statue!" Rachael looked at Marigold with wide eyes. In fact, all three other witchy ladies did, too.

"What?" Marigold looked between them.

"Where were you last night?" Rachael's voice was an octave lower than it had been. Serious. All eyes moved to a long counter along the back wall of the café. "Wait, where is your Destiny Goddess Statue?" Rachael's tone became even lower.

"I took it home. Last week. I didn't do this to Maple May. I didn't!"

"Well, if not you, who?" Rachael asked, her voice getting louder and louder with each accusation.

Marigold motioned at me with her chin. "She's the one that told us it looked like the statue!"

I pulled back. "I don't even know what this destiny statue is. I certainly don't own one!"

Marigold shook her head back and forth for several seconds. She finally spoke to the others in a low, desperate voice. "You have to believe me. I didn't do this, but someone is trying to make this look like it's my fault!"

Chapter Six

THE FOUR LADIES TALKED over each other nonstop after I laid out the napkin reenactment. I couldn't understand much of what they were saying—only that Marigold Weathers was known for using something called a Destiny Goddess Statue for spiritual sensing, and all three others believed that Maple May's legs had been placed in that position purposefully, and she hadn't simply fallen in that direction after being struck with a car.

As they spoke over one another, all I could think of was my dream—with Brendan and the other realtors "staging" the scene of Maple May's death with throw pillows. Had my subconscious known all along that there was something purposeful about the details of Maple May's death?

"I should talk to Detective Jameson," Rachael said, and they nodded, all except for Marigold, who suddenly seemed busy with something on her phone. I recognized Jameson as a name Detective Thom had mentioned last night.

I wondered if I should mention it, but if these witches were saying they suspected a possible murder, the last thing I wanted was to get me or my last name involved in it. Especially because they all kept eyeing me sidelong, as though they still didn't fully believe my ignorance regarding Destiny Goddess Statues.

"Listen, I should really go. I have a lot of work to do on my aunt's boat." I snapped my mouth shut the second the words were out, remembering I wasn't supposed to mention my relation to my aunt. Thankfully, the four women were so caught up in the scandal of Maple May's death, they failed to notice.

"Please do come back Wednesday night, if you're still in town." Marigold smiled up at me, as if automatically turning on her charm again, as I stepped away. It sounded almost like an afterthought, so I nodded with a small smile, deciding not to argue.

When I brought my mug back up to the counter, Avrum asked, "What did you think of the lavender latte?"

I frowned down at my mostly full cup. "I'm afraid I let most of it go cold when I got busy talking."

Avrum looked toward the back of the café and his jaw tightened. He muttered a few words that sounded like "Those witches did it again," before turning back to me and offering a smile. "Well, then I suppose you'll have to come in for another, won't you?"

I definitely planned to—perhaps one to-go on my way out of town.

I retraced my steps toward the marina, thinking again about how friendly and outgoing the people of

Crystal Cove were—or certainly would have been, if they didn't have mysterious details of a friend's death on their minds. The sidewalks had gotten busier with pedestrians since I stopped in for coffee, and every single one of them said hello to me during my short three-block walk.

I breathed in the fresh sea air as I arrived at the dock. After stopping to put my umbrella back into my car, I took a quick look at the front edge of the hood. There no longer seemed to be any traces of blood, but I'd brought a bucket of cleaners along to give a once-over to the boat, so I popped my trunk and sprayed some disinfectant over the whole front of my car anyway. I wiped it off with a dry rag, thankful for once that my car was an old model on its last legs and I didn't have to worry about ruining the paint.

Now, in the daylight and after having a few sips of coffee, I took note of more details about the marina. While my aunt's boat wasn't visible from the entry to the main wharf, several wooden signs marked the way to the Lady of Fortune. My mom always gave me the impression that Aunt Lizzie wasn't hurting for money or clients, but the state of her boat and even the faded signage suggested otherwise.

Along with the other nearby boats, I also now glimpsed what looked like a floating shack to my right. On a worn wooden sign above the door was one carved word: OFFICE.

I had to stand at a distance from the door to knock, trying not to lose my balance from the gap between the shack and the wharf. There was no answer. I knocked again and called out, "Hello?"

A man rounded the cabin on a nearby sailboat. "Hi! What can I do for ya?"

"Are you the manager around here?" I motioned to the marina.

"Sure am." He wore a plaid shirt and jeans that looked to be covered in a mixture of grease and dirt. He offered a big grin. "Name's Frank. Are you here for a tour?"

"A tour?" I looked around at the nearby boats, wondering which ones were for hired tours. I'd once gone on a lovely sunset dinner cruise with Reiger Realty employees at Christmas, but none of these looked big enough for something like that. Besides, it was barely one in the afternoon. "No, actually, I'm here on behalf of the Lady of Fortune. I'm here to fix it up and sell it."

Frank looked down at his greasy hands and nodded, going instantly somber. When he looked up again, he asked, "You Lizzie's family then?"

It was all I could do to tell a lie to this man who looked honest and vulnerable. "I've been hired by the family." Before I could let the callousness of my words sit in the air for too long, I went on. "Do you know if it's actually classified as a houseboat? And do you have any idea of the channels where such a boat might be advertised?"

Frank looked off into the distance, even though the Lady of Fortune wasn't in our view. By his pensive gaze, I could tell he was picturing it. "It's a bit of a hybrid, Lizzie's boat," he told me. "'Fraid there's not much market right now for anything much other than motorboats or them big yachts." He shrugged. "I suppose you could try putting up some flyers around town. Maybe for the right price someone would pick it up for sentimental reasons."

A few things were wrong with that statement. First, shouldn't my parents be the ones wanting to keep it for sentimental reasons? But I knew their story well, by this point. They—or at least Dad—had no emotions when it came to holding onto anything that might hurt his reputation. The scarcity of possible buyers also bothered me, as did the words "right price." Dad had told me more than once that a boat like Aunt Lizzie's should bring in a couple hundred thousand dollars—which was why I had immediately assumed it belonged on the housing market. The boat I'd seen last night, it couldn't be worth ten thousand, at least the way it was now.

"Okay, well, thank you for your help, Frank."

"You bet. Let me know if I can help with anything. And if you do sell, be sure to let me know. There's a one-month notice policy on mooring at Crystal Marina."

I wondered if I should just give him the notice right now. But I decided that conversation could wait for the moment. Maybe once I told Dad what this boat was really worth and how difficult it might be to sell, he'd consider at least keeping it for Mom's sentimentality.

When I got to the wharf that led to the Lady of Fortune, I immediately saw a tall blond man leaning from the wharf and looking through a window on the side of my aunt's boat.

"Can I help you with something?" I asked, walking closer. As I did, I couldn't help but notice how well the man filled out a pair of jeans and a lavender T-shirt that perfectly matched my coffee topping from this morning. He looked like he worked out.

He turned and a smile erupted onto his wildly attractive face. I'd always been a sucker for dimples on men and this guy had them in spades. He blinked, and I swore I felt a waft of wind from his thick eyelashes. This man was magazine-worthy. "Sure, yeah, probably," he said, and his voice was as buttery smooth as I expected from such a face. "Are you the lady selling this boat?"

I raised my eyebrows. "Wow, word travels fast in a small town." He couldn't have heard the news from Frank, as I'd only just finished speaking to him. Had he spoken to one of the witches at the café and then beat me here? There was no other explanation. "I haven't had a chance to really fix it up yet, but yes. It will be for sale soon."

Maybe Frank was mistaken. Maybe folks would be clamoring for such a strange hybrid of a boat. I just hoped this guy wouldn't ask for a price, at least not before I could clean it up a bit and talk it over with my dad.

"You selling the stuff inside, too?" He glanced back to the window he'd been peering through.

I squinted. Most of the interior had looked pretty dilapidated. "Is there something specific you're looking for?"

The man shrugged. "Lizzie had a nice crystal ball. Maybe some crystals. I'm specifically on the lookout for some small blue crystals."

At the reminder, I fingered the small blue glass trinket in my coat pocket. But that hadn't come from my aunt's boat. I'd found it on the roadside, so I didn't pull it out or mention it. Even though his voice remained casual, something about this man rang false. Growing up with a politician who was always campaigning gave me a keen eye for that sort of thing.

"I, uh, I'll have to talk to the family to see what they want to sell and what they'll keep." I felt my cheeks warm—I wasn't sure if it was a delayed reaction to this man's attractiveness or a result of my half-truths.

"Oh. You're not family?"

My face flush intensified. To hide it, I turned toward the door of the boat, stepped aboard, and let the purple drapes cover me for a second while I unlocked it with my key. "I'm, um, here to get it up for sale on their behalf."

When I turned back, the man gave me a side-eye for about a half second and then outstretched his hand. "I'm Jay, by the way. And you are?"

I felt like he already knew who I was. I couldn't explain quite why. I wrote it off as a small-town thing. I reached across the gap of water, and as I did, my aunt's cat came racing out the door of the boat's cabin and between me and Jay, launching himself over the gap of water as though he was born taking such risks with his short little legs.

I knew for a fact that I'd put the cat outside when I left for coffee. Now I was the one looking at Jay sidelong. Had he somehow been inside? Was that why he knew about the crystal ball on the table and my aunt's other possessions?

"Tabitha," I said eventually, retracting my hand.

He chuckled. "Tabby and her tabby, huh?"

I didn't get what he meant until he motioned toward where my aunt's cat now rounded the corner onto the next wharf.

"Not mine," I started to explain. But then it hit me. I guessed the cat actually was mine, at least until I found another home for him. I hated to admit it, but it wasn't the most unwelcome thought in the world, even if I'd have to sneak him into my pet-less apartment building.

"And you say you're not family?" he asked again. I avoided his eyes and pretended to straighten the wrought iron chairs on the front deck. When I didn't answer, he asked, "Do you know anyone else here in Crystal Cove?"

He made me feel exactly how that Detective Thom had last night and even how the witches in the café had made me feel—like I had done something wrong, even though I knew I had not.

"How did you say you heard the boat and its contents were for sale?"

"I didn't," Jay answered with a wink. "You just got into town last night, right?"

I didn't appreciate the wink. I got the distinct impression he was playing games with me. If only I could tell him I was here mourning my dead aunt and trying to appease my father, all while trying to keep the first job I could be proud of in Portland. I didn't need people chattering on about me behind my back. "That's right. Just here for a couple of days to fix up the boat and get it up for sale." I wondered if Frank would be willing to show the boat to any tourists passing through who might be interested after I left.

"I suspect this here vessel might need more than a couple of days' worth of work."

The truth of his statement frustrated me. "Right. Well, if you're not interested in buying it, I'm afraid I'd better get to work."

"But you didn't take down my information."

I looked at him quizzically.

"In case you want to chat more about selling the knickknacks from inside?"

"Oh. Right." I pulled out my phone, ready to make a show of taking down his number, now even more certain that I didn't want to sell my aunt's precious items to this shifty guy who seemed to have more going on under the surface.

But instead, he reached across the water to hand me a business card. "Give me a call if you find any blue crystals while cleaning up the boat or if you want to discuss anything at all during your visit here to Crystal Cove."

He turned and walked away, and my eyes betrayed me, wanting to watch the perfect fit of his jeans descending the dock. It wasn't until he was out of sight that I looked down at his name on the business card in my hand.

Jay Jameson.

Detective Jay Jameson.

No wonder I'd felt like I was being interrogated all over again.

Chapter Seven

ALL AFTERNOON, AS I scrubbed walls and floors and collected what I guessed to be my aunt's most precious items into a box to take with me, I thought about Jay Jameson.

Why hadn't he introduced himself as a detective? Why question me under false pretenses, only to give me a card at the end of our conversation that revealed his true identity? Did that mean he had decided I wasn't involved in the hit-and-run or was it a ploy to keep me off balance? He'd kept asking after my aunt's wares—was he truly interested in buying them or could they somehow be involved in his investigation?

I thought again about Marigold's and Rachael's upset over Maple May's death. How they'd thought it had been intentional because of a similarity between the body's position and some sort of destiny statue.

Could my aunt own one of those statues? I hadn't come across one yet, but she had about a million knickknacks and I'd barely sorted through the ones on display. Was that the kind of information Detective Jameson had been prying for? Rachael, the witch with the striped tights, had talked about calling a Detective Jameson—and so had Detective Thom for that matter.

I had a sick feeling about this, no matter which way I put it together, because maybe Detective Thom wasn't the only one in town becoming increasingly convinced that my family and I were somehow responsible for Maple May's death.

Dad called me from home later that evening, and my sick feeling multiplied. I tried to stick to the facts of why I was here.

"The boat's in bad shape, Dad. It probably won't garner the kind of price you're looking for."

The politician in him was on full display as he told me, "I'm in the middle of a very expensive campaign, Tabby. I know you have the family's best interests in mind, and with your talent as a realtor, you'll be sure to get a good price for it."

Whenever my father complimented me, which was not often, I couldn't seem to find any kind of argument, even if what he said was dead wrong. "Can I talk to Mom?"

He passed the phone over. Before I left for Crystal Cove, my father had warned me multiple times how hard this had all been on my mom and that the quicker I could handle the sale and the less I had to discuss the details about it with her, the better. But I was still rattled by Detective Jameson's visit and at the very least I wanted to know what I should and shouldn't sell.

"How's everything going down there, Tabby?" Mom asked when she got on the phone. Her voice was more chipper than I expected. "Dad said you had a bit of car trouble, but you got it all worked out?"

Ha. A bit of car trouble was what he called it? But who was I kidding? If I'd been able to come up with a seamless excuse like that one, I would have used it in a second. "Yes, I think it's worked out. Hey, listen . . ." As Aunt Lizzie's cat jumped up to sit on the loveseat beside me, I figured why not start with that. "Any idea what I should do with Aunt Lizzie's cat?"

Mom sighed. "I'd hate to give Sherlock to the pound. Can you find a new home for him in town there? Or are you allowed cats in your apartment?"

When my dad had gone apartment shopping with me, he'd assured me that places that accepted pets would all smell awful, so I was pretty sure it didn't. I'd never considered owning a pet, so it hadn't been an issue. But I had to admit, the idea was growing on me.

"Maybe," I told her, envisioning myself sneaking the squat cat through the building lobby in my suitcase. I looked down at the cat as he wriggled his nose to push his glasses up. I loved that his name was Sherlock, and I glanced again at Lizzie's shelf of detective novels. "Hey, anything else of Aunt Lizzie's you know you want to hang onto? I wanted to pack up all of her most precious things to bring home before I do an overhaul on the boat."

Mom's voice became somber. "She had a lot of friends in town. Anything you can rehome to someone she knew, that would be fine with me. Just . . . use your own judgment."

Right. My own judgment. That would be fine if I was sitting back in Portland, not looking at every item that all of a sudden seemed sentimental. I hated being responsible for this part of it.

But I didn't let my confusion show to Mom and said goodbye. After hanging up, I scratched Sherlock's fur around his neck, and he immediately purred in response. I had to admit, even though I had never considered myself a cat person, this cat really did bring comfort. He made me feel less alone.

He had a collar around his neck, which turned as I ruffled his fur. The heart-shaped tag had a little blue jewel in it. I peered closer and then grabbed for my coat, which I'd thrown over a kitchen chair. Sure enough, I pulled out the small blue jewel that I'd found near the scene of the accident last night, and it was an exact match.

Sherlock let out a loud meow and swatted at my hand that held the jewel, almost knocking it away from me.

"Hey, hey!" I said. "Calm down."

But he continued nosing at the jewel, and that's when I noticed the tiny hole in the middle of his glasses. On a lark, I pressed the blue jewel into the hole, and it was a perfect fit.

Ah, that's better. Thank you! a voice in my head said.

I looked around the small boat cabin, but there was no one else around. Was it my aunt's ghost? No, I reminded myself. I didn't believe in ghosts.

"Hello?" I called out nevertheless. I attempted to say it to the boat cabin but then picked up Sherlock and stared through his glasses into his eyes.

This time when I heard a voice, I felt the vibration of it in my hands. I'm right here, silly. Now tell me what you found at that coffee shop.

Chapter Eight

IN AN INSTANT, RABIES and sharp claws were the least of my worries. I launched the cat away from me, jumped up off the loveseat, and took two giant steps away from him.

That could not have just happened. My mind was clearly exhausted from the stress of the last twenty-four hours.

Oh dear, the voice in my head said. I stared at the cat, but his mouth wasn't moving. Master said this might happen.

I paced back and forth in the small cabin. I shook my head violently, trying to clear it. Then I headed for the outside door. I probably just needed some air.

I let the door fall shut behind me and sucked in two giant breaths of fresh sea air. Ahh, that was better.

But then I felt something rub up against my ankles, and I knew what it was before I looked down. "Aunt Lizzie?" I asked in barely a whisper.

The cat looked up at me and tilted his head.

Okay, yes. I'd had this wrong. Inside and among my aunt's wares, it was easy to think I was hearing things, but out here, my head was clear. There were no figments of my imagination out here.

Are you better now? Can we talk about your morning?

I blinked my eyes shut and held them there for a long moment. The figments of my imagination weren't stopping, even in the fresh air.

I shook my head and backed all the way up against the rail at the front of the deck. "You can't be a talking cat. You can't!" I whisper-hissed. I should have felt relieved that the voice didn't appear to be actually coming from the cat, but instead I could only worry about my mental health.

I headed back inside since the fresh air didn't appear to be helping. I sidestepped the crystal ball on the table as I went past and headed straight for the door to the upper deck and my aunt's bedroom, hoping the cat—and the voice—couldn't follow me there.

He didn't. Moments later, I sat on my aunt's purple paisley bedspread alone. But that didn't make me feel any better. I took in a deep yoga breath and pursed my lips to push it out slowly. Aunt Lizzie always used to tell me not to be afraid of the supernatural, to lean into it to find my own special gifting. As an eight-year-old, I hadn't understood what that meant, but I didn't think I had been afraid of much back then, so that sounded fun.

"But what if I don't believe in it anymore?" I asked the air around me. "Why now? When you're gone and you can't help me figure it out?"

I was only greeted with silence.

I lay back and tried to enjoy a few minutes of quiet, tried to let my stressful thoughts fall away. But they didn't. If anything, they multiplied. My dad had sent me off to do the impossible. It would take a miracle to fix up this boat in two days and sell it for the kind of money he was looking for. I wasn't ready to be a disappointment to him again.

Then I thought again of Detective Jameson showing up at the boat to interrogate me. I was clearly still a suspect in the hit-and-run of a young witch, and I was sure it didn't look innocent to the police that I was the niece of a local fortune-teller.

On top of that, I had to worry about my mental health because I was hearing voices.

I just felt so alone in all of it. I laughed at the thought because the voices and that cat might have been the only parts of this that didn't make me feel alone.

They only made me feel crazy.

Ten minutes of deliberating and I decided that yes, crazy was better than alone. I pushed up from my aunt's bed and headed back down to the lower deck. During that short time, Sherlock had curled up on the loveseat and closed his eyes, but he immediately made me feel less alone, regardless. In fact, I felt a lot more clearheaded than I had a few minutes ago.

The police were looking for crystals? The least I could do was start cleaning up Aunt Lizzie's things and see if I could find any. Maybe if I could provide some for Detective Jameson, that would somehow prove my innocence.

I'd brought a stack of flattened cardboard boxes along with me from Portland. I hauled those in from my car, sat cross-legged on the floor of the boat, and began to fold some together. When I had a half dozen put together, I reached over for the bottom drawers in Aunt Lizzie's bureau and started to empty them.

I figured I'd have one box for things I wanted to keep and five for items to give away to any locals who may have known Lizzie, but as I pulled out scarves and jewelry, I could picture each one on my Aunt Lizzie and the box of stuff to keep got fuller and fuller and eventually, I had to start a second one.

A few minutes later, I looked over and was surprised to see that Sherlock had relocated himself and he now slept peacefully inside one of the empty boxes. Seeing him there made me smile, and without thinking, I said, "A cute talking cat wouldn't be the worst thing in the world, I suppose."

An immediate voice came into my head. Master was right. Humans are funny about what they will and won't believe.

"Humans? And then . . . what are you?" I stared at the only other living being I knew to be aboard this houseboat.

The cat waggled his eyebrows at me, but my head remained silent.

I had to be clear about what my mind thought it was hearing though. "So . . . you're a cat?"

The cat readjusted his head on his front paws, but again, I didn't hear any words.

Mental instability or not, I couldn't seem to stop this conversation or whatever it was with this cat. I thought back to the unsettling conversation I'd had with Detective Jameson. "I'm a Tabby, too. Though some people call me a Tabitha."

The cat meowed, as if saying hello.

"Who's your master?"

This time, it wasn't a voice in my head, but a vision: my Aunt Lizzie twirling with her bright orange skirt and multi-colored scarves flying out in every direction. The bright smile on her face and the twinkle in her eye gave me a renewed pang of missing her.

The cat let out a louder, sadder mreow—this one using his mouth—and somehow I knew it meant he missed her, too.

"I— She was my aunt. We were related," I added, not knowing how much cats understood about human relationships. Even though I didn't have full assurance that this cat could understand a word I said, it made me feel better to say these things out loud.

"She . . . she died. About a month ago. Did you know that?"

The cat tilted his head at me. I suspected he either didn't understand death or thought nine lives applied to humans. My mother had had to drive down to Crystal Cove to identify her half-sister's body, but those were details I didn't want to say aloud.

What about the coffee shop? came into my head.

I thought of it as a café, rather than a coffee shop, so either I was developing a multiple personality disorder or the voice I was hearing was not mine.

"How do you know I found anything at the coffee shop?" I asked aloud. "How did you even know I went to a coffee shop?"

Sherlock lifted a front paw and licked it, which looked like a shrug in cat language. Sometimes I know things.

"Right. So you're psychic on top of everything else?" I got up from the floor and moved an empty box onto the bureau to load the detective novels into. At least these I could give away without any guilt. But when silence fell over the boat again, I decided I didn't like it.

"And if you knew that I'd find something out at The Heirloom Café, don't you think it might have helped to mention it before I went there?" I muttered, as if to myself. "Why didn't we have this conversation this morning?" I shook my head at the word conversation.

Sherlock got up and hopped out of the empty box. He padded to the kitchen, hopped up on his hind legs, and pulled open the cupboard to reveal the empty coffee can. Was he trying to say he had tried to tell me?

I sighed, placed my first full box of detective novels onto the floor, and then picked up another empty one to fill. Before I had the next box half full, the cat meowed up at me. I looked down, and he was perched on the spines of the detective novels inside the first box, pawing at one in particular. These ones were hardcover, which helped with him keeping his balance.

"You like detective novels?" The more I spoke of everyday stuff, the more used to talking out loud to an animal I became. I bent and pulled at the novel he'd been pawing at. He moved aside to let me get it out.

The second it was out on the floor, I watched with interest as the cat not only opened the cover of the novel but began flipping pages. He landed on one he seemed to like and bent to peer closer at it, so his glasses were practically touching the page of written words in front of him.

"No." I shook my head. "Surely, you can't read."

He pulled back, flipped another few pages, and then bent close to the page once more. I thought again about the crystal I'd inserted into his eyeglasses. That had seemingly made the difference and caused the voices in my head.

Hmm. I reached over and pulled at the elastic strap on the back of his head to release the glasses. They came off easily, but a second later, Sherlock backed away from the book, lay down with his head on his front paws, and looked like he was going back to sleep.

"Can you hear what I'm saying? If you can, meow," I told the cat.

He ignored me, eyes shut.

I peered through one lens of the glasses and then the other. If they had any prescription at all, it was very low. I pulled the elastic and placed the glasses back onto the cat's face. He blinked his eyes open, stood, and padded back over to the open detective novel. He promptly brought his face right up against the page again.

"If you can hear what I'm saying now, meow," I told him for a second time.

This time, he looked right at me and let out a loud, drawn-out meowwwww.

Right. So this cat, this nonhuman feline species, seemed to be able to understand and even talk to me when his glasses were in place. Specifically, when the blue crystal was in place. And this was a blue crystal I'd found out near a dead witch I'd come across in the middle of the road. I really was going crazy. I took another deep yoga breath to help me process.

But finally I had to ask. "Can you read actual English words, too?" When he only looked up at me, but I didn't hear any kind of answer, I told him, "Meow if you can actually read those words."

He looked back at the page, peered closely at it, but didn't let out a single sound.

Okay, at least that was one bit of crazy I didn't have to get my mind past. But as he flipped more pages and continued leaning in practically against the pages, a thought came to me. "Would you like me to read it to you?"

He immediately backed away and looked up at me. Yes, please.

I picked up the book and looked at the cover. The Mystery of the Missing Statue. This made me think again about Marigold Weathers and the Destiny Goddess Statue she had taken home with her. The same one that supposedly was in the same shape that Maple May's body had been left in.

I leaned into the page Sherlock had been studying and read from the top.

"And when was the last time you saw your statue?" the detective asked.

"It was right here in my foyer only two nights ago," the woman said.

I read several more paragraphs, all questions about the value, dimensions, and appearance of the statue in question. It soon became clear that the statue in the novel was much larger and held the shape of a bird, rather than some type of humanlike goddess.

I stopped reading and looked down at Sherlock. "Marigold Weathers spoke today about a Destiny Goddess Statue." When Sherlock stared up at me but didn't seem to show recognition, I went on and explained the body I'd seen on the road last night and how it had been formed into the same shape as this statue.

Missing statue? came into my mind.

I nodded. "You might be right. Maybe it is now missing."

What is a Marigold Weathers?

I smiled at the phrasing. Every time I got some assurance the voices in my head weren't my own type of crazy, it made me feel a little better. And at the same time a little worse. "Marigold is a local witch. She has purple hair—"

Ahh, yes, the purple witch. He lay down on his front paws again. Time to ask her about the missing statue, then.

Chapter Nine

I WENT TO BED that night convinced that I was not about to go chasing a purple-haired witch around Crystal Cove, looking for a missing statue. Let the police deal with it. Surely they would quickly realize that I was simply an innocent out-of-town visitor who had nothing to do with any supernatural crimes.

Even if I had somehow started to develop my own strange ability to talk to cats.

Cat, I reminded myself. Not that the singularity of my ability made it any better.

As I child, I'd wanted to believe my Aunt Lizzie had some kind of special powers, but as I grew older, I'd come to accept my parents' point of view: she was an aging lady who had a knack for reading people's body language. But now I had to wonder . . . Had my aunt been able to communicate with Sherlock, too?

This, no matter which way you swung it, was more than reading body language.

I fell asleep reading the detective novel Sherlock had been so interested in and awoke the next morning during another strange dream. This one was a short snippet of the dead witch, Maple May, but she was spinning like how I'd pictured my Aunt Lizzie. Maple May was sleeker than my aunt had been, in her jeans and yellow poncho, and strikingly beautiful, but what really caught my attention was a sparkling comb tucked into her hair. The blue jewels in the comb looked brilliant against her now-dry strawberry-blonde hair.

Jewels or . . . crystals?

I sat up in bed, trying to catch my breath. Were there blue crystals out at the scene of Maple May's death because she'd worn some out there? Did she have some sort of magical abilities from them, too? And did Detective Jameson suspect Aunt Lizzie may have had some more of the crystals on her boat or did he suspect I'd taken some from the crime scene?

I left my aunt's bedroom assured of one thing: I had to know if there were more blue crystals aboard the boat. I'd deal with my warring thoughts about whether or not to tell the police about the two that Sherlock was wearing later.

By the time I emptied the bureau, I had three full boxes of items to keep, but I hadn't found a single other blue crystal. I'd been pointedly trying to contain myself from talking to the cat, even though he had been pawing at the empty coffee can all morning.

Finally, as I finished with the bureau, I turned to him and sighed. "You think I should go for coffee again?" As much as I didn't want to admit it, getting out of here for a cup of coffee was exactly what I needed right now.

I just hoped doing so would subtract from the drama in my life, rather than add to it.

"So back to the café," I said. Sherlock sat up on his haunches at attention. "Apparently they hold a witch's group there on Wednesdays, and yesterday I met four of the witches."

Sherlock did his whisker waggling thing. The purple witch?

"Marigold Weathers? Yes. She seems like the highest-ranking witch in town." I supposed I was getting comfortable talking out loud to him again, wasn't I? That sure didn't take long. "And the other three wanted to blame her for the witch I'd seen dead on the road last night."

Dead witch?

I didn't know if he'd forgotten me telling him about her yesterday or if he just wanted more description. "Maple May Doerksen," I told him. "She was young, about my age, with reddish-blonde hair, and she wore a yellow poncho. The police thought I had hit her with my car, but I didn't. The witches thought Maple May's body was placed on the road in the position of the Destiny Goddess Statue that Marigold owns, and they didn't think Maple May's death was an accident."

Murder! The ominous voice in my head made me pause from where I was picking up my coat to put it on.

Was this truly a murder? And could Maple May have truly been wearing blue crystals when it happened?

Look up! Statue!

I stared up at the plain white ceiling of the boat, but then Sherlock started pawing at my coat pocket where I kept my phone.

"Oh. Right." I pulled out my phone and searched the words "Destiny Goddess Statue" in my browser. Seconds later, several articles popped up, but I skipped over those and clicked on the images tab at the top. The second they loaded, I sucked in a breath. "This is exactly what her body looked like!" I said.

Sherlock lay down on his front paws as though this whole investigation was making him tired. Then he started purring.

I wanted to know more, so I pulled out my laptop and sat at the table, waiting for it to boot up. The crystal ball didn't give me a lot of room, but I also hadn't quite gotten my mind around moving it. With a talking cat, who knew what else might come to life on this boat if I fiddled too much with my aunt's magical wares?

I looked over to where Sherlock was snuggling back into an empty box, despite my padding around and digging into my bags for my computer.

As I waited for my laptop to connect with my phone's hotspot, I thought again about Detective Jay Jameson. I didn't like the fact that he'd hidden his identity from me, but it wasn't as though I felt friendly with Detective Thom either. And why had both Detective Thom and Rachael-of-the-black-and-white-striped-tights suggested calling Detective Jameson on this case? Rachael had mentioned him right after they'd discussed the body shape on the road. I wondered, with the detective's curiosity about my aunt's fortune-telling wares, if he might be a lot more familiar with them than I was.

I ran a finger over his business card as my laptop finally connected and my browser came to life.

My intention had been to research Destiny Goddess Statues, but now that I was staring at my computer, I had another idea. I opened a blank spreadsheet and logged in every suspicious thing I'd come across since arriving in Crystal Cove—from the concrete items, such as the blue crystal I'd found at the scene of Maple May's death, to the more abstract, such as the thoughts I suspected were coming from the cat and my strange dreams.

Beside each item, I listed anyone who may know more about it or where I could do more research. Most came down to the four witches I'd met yesterday.

To try to get my mind off this, I tabbed back over to my browser and typed in

"How to sell a houseboat."

Thousands of answers appeared—everything from sales websites to Wiki-How pages on how to stage a houseboat to prepare for selling. Even though I was Reiger Realty's most prepared when it came to staging houses, I clicked on an entry, figuring I had a lot to learn about boats.

I wasn't wrong. I wouldn't have even considered jobs like waxing the hull or checking the color of the motor's oil, but those were among the first items listed. I started a second spreadsheet and made another list as I scoured website after website.

The spreadsheets made me feel more in control, like this whole situation wasn't getting away from me. It was what I did for a living at home—researched and organized information on each house I was assigned to help with.

I could handle most of the interior staging on the boat, but two hours later, when it was well past time for a coffee and a muffin, I figured I'd see if Frank was around on my way off the wharf, as he was the closest person I had come into contact with who might be an expert when it came to boats.

Sherlock barely stirred as I locked up the boat, and this time I didn't kick him out. Hopefully, with his new communication skills, he would let me know if he thought he'd need to go out to the bathroom. Or who knew? Maybe he'd learned how to use the one on the boat.

Frank was right where I'd found him yesterday, hands greasy and working on the same sailboat, but this time he saw me coming.

"Good morning!" he called with a greasy wave. "Tabitha, right?"

I nodded and checked my watch. Sure enough, it was still morning but barely. "Good morning. Hey, Frank, I'm trying to research more about the make of my aunt's boat and the year and some of the interior fixtures. Any idea how I'd figure out more about those things?"

Frank shrugged. "There should be a latch somewhere near the helm, just like on a car. It should have the registration papers and all that."

I nodded, making a note on my phone. I assumed the helm was that little area near the front with the steering wheel that I'd had yet to explore. "I see you're busy working on boats around here, and I wondered if you're available for hire? I have to get the motor and exterior of my aunt's boat ready for sale, and I'm a little out of my depth there, so to speak."

"Between this and my upcoming tours, I'm going to be tied up for a while." He motioned to the boat he'd been working on for the last two days. "But I could ask my nephew, if ya like. He's been taking classes in mechanics and bodywork, and he's always on the lookout for vehicles to work on. I'd bet with a boat, he'd help you out for free."

Free was definitely the best price. But could I trust this nephew who was still learning?

As if Frank could sense my deliberation, he added, "Don't worry.

Dave does pretty good work, and I'll check it all over for ya, if you'd like."

I nodded hesitantly.

"I'll get him to come by and have a gander right away."

I glanced toward town. "I was just about to grab a coffee and a muffin. Can you ask him to come by in about an hour?"

Frank winked. "Just grab me a cuppa Avrum's star anise brew, and I'll take care of it."

As I said goodbye and walked up toward town, I decided maybe this was simply things working out for me for a change. If Frank was willing to check over his nephew's work, what did I have to worry about?

Although now that I thought about it, I'd only met Frank yesterday. What did I know about the guy?

By the time I reached The Heirloom Café, my mouth was watering for another lavender latte. The café was a lot quieter today, with Avrum behind the counter stirring up something in a mixing bowl and Rachael in the upper corner where she had been yesterday, but today she was alone and hunched over her cup. I only recognized her by her striped tights.

"What can I get for you today?" Avrum asked, taking my attention. He had so much dark hair that I wondered if it shouldn't be in a hairnet. Then again, in such a small town, health inspectors probably didn't come by often.

"I'd love another lavender latte. And a cup of star anise brew," I added, trying to remember if that was exactly the way Frank had worded it.

"I'm afraid I'm all out of the lavender," he said. "But I've got a cardamom coffee on special if you'd like to try?"

That didn't sound as appealing. "Isn't that lavender?" I pointed to a jar on the back counter that looked like it was filled with yet-to-be-crushed lavender stalks.

"Oh. Yeah. But that's my personal stash and it's not ground yet." He rubbed his temples. "I get stress headaches, and I like to avoid taking Tylenol if I can help it. Plus, grinding the spices relaxes me. Sometimes I do it at home in the evenings, in front of the TV."

"Have you tried mint on your temples?" I asked. My mom had been using that on me and my siblings since we were kids.

"No, I'll have to look into that," he said.

"Why don't you make it two star anise brews?" Frank seemed to know what he liked. I was willing to give his favorite a try.

Avrum nodded and got to work making them. After mentioning that these orders were to go, I headed up to Rachael to pepper her with a few questions about statues and crystals. Even though I kept telling myself I wasn't going to get involved, I couldn't seem to stop thinking about all my questions.

"Hey? Rachael?" I said when I was a few feet away and she hadn't heard me.

She looked up and her face was streaked with tears. Her eyes were bloodshot as though she'd been crying a long time.

"Is everything okay?" I moved closer and put a hand on her shoulder.

She started to nod but then shook her head. "I should be able to figure this out, but I just can't!"

"Should be able to figure what out?" I took the seat across from her, wondering where all her friends were today and why Avrum hadn't even seemed to have noticed her sitting up here crying her eyes out.

"Maple May and what happened to her. I feel like it's on the tip of my tongue, but no matter what I try, I can't get the answer."

"Well, what have you tried?" Hopefully something a little more normal than talking to her pets. "Did you talk to that detective?"

She shook her head. "He couldn't tell me anything. But I also sensed he didn't know anything, which only makes me feel more pressure to figure it out."

Why would she feel the pressure? "I'm sure the police will solve it." My words were greeted with an unbelieving scowl. Rachael clearly had no faith in the police's investigative ability.

"They're going to write it off as a hit-and-run. I just know it!" It seemed my trying to comfort her was only making her more upset, which made me feel awful.

"Where are your friends? Have you spoken to them about this?"

She looked at me blankly.

"The other . . . witches?" It came out as a whisper. I still hadn't wrapped my mind around there being an actual coven of witches in this town.

"Oh, believe me, they're not my friends. Every witch in this town is out for themselves, and now that I've started poking blame about Maple May's death, they've all suddenly disappeared."

"Do you really think Marigold did something to hurt Maple May?" I asked. Even if her body was in a strange position, I was still more apt to think it had been a hit-and-run. But I wanted to have compassion if Rachael was having trouble accepting that. "Did you find out where that statue of hers went?"

Rachael's eyes widened. "You're right! That's what I should do—go to her house and see if she has her Destiny Goddess Statue or if she was lying about that!" I hadn't exactly suggested that, and I momentarily worried that another witch in this town might end up hurt or dead, but before I could caution Rachael, she said, "Something isn't adding up, and all of a sudden, none of the others want to talk to me about it. It's up to me to figure out what's going on, and I have to do it before Wednesday."

"Wednesday?" I asked, right as Avrum called, "Tabitha? Your order is ready."

Had I told him my name? As I stood, Rachael reminded me, "Witchy Wednesday. I know none of them would miss that. I just have to have something about Maple May's death figured out by then, so I can confront them and tell the rest of the witches in town." With her words, she looked resolute.

She stared down at the table, and that was when I saw she had reconstructed my napkin diagram of how Maple May's body had looked.

I sensed she was singly focused now more than she was upset. But I still felt guilty about spurring her on toward the other witches, and I didn't want this girl to get hurt. "Well, if you need a friend, you can find me at the marina at my aunt's boat." I snapped my mouth shut. It was the second time I'd accidentally mentioned my relationship to my aunt.

But Rachael nodded and barely seemed to notice my words. As I backed away to get my coffee, I got the sense she wasn't just distracted. She was going into some kind of trance.

And I definitely didn't want to be here for that!

Chapter Ten

THE COFFEES WERE STILL warm in my hands by the time I got back to the marina, but mine was already half gone. Frank knew what he was talking about when it came to coffee orders. I would have never thought of grinding star anise up as a coffee flavoring, but it worked perfectly to augment the bitterness.

"Frank?" I called when I got near his shack. But this time there was no response. I'd probably have a hard time resisting drinking both coffees if he wasn't around, even though I didn't need that much caffeine.

After a few minutes of looking around his shack and the boat he'd been working on earlier, I sighed and gave up. I headed for my aunt's boat, and it wasn't until I rounded the corner onto her wharf that I found out why Frank wasn't at his usual station.

Apparently, his nephew Dave had shown up early, and the two of them were crouched down on the wharf, discussing the Lady of Fortune.

From a distance, Dave didn't appear to be the picture of knowledge or trustworthiness. His dirty jeans hung low on his hips, showing half his underwear, and his dark hair looked about as greasy as his Uncle Frank's hands.

Great. What had I agreed to?

I moved closer and had more to worry about. Dave didn't look like he could even be fifteen years old. When Frank said he was taking classes for mechanics, I had just assumed some kind of trade college, not high school.

"Oh, hey! Is that my coffee?" When Frank stood and motioned to my hand, I realized how long I'd probably been standing there with my stunned thoughts. "I was just telling Dave about the dead witch you saw on your way into town."

I didn't recall telling Frank about the tragedy I'd encountered two nights ago. I supposed I had to chalk that up to small-town gossip, along with the barista knowing my name. I passed the coffee over, trying to coax some words to reply to Frank's blunt statement, but it turned out, I didn't need to because his nephew piped up and they carried the conversation all on their own.

"If you ask me, one of those crazy witches cast a spell on the other and killed their own," Dave said. "Their fights are some of the biggest excitement this town has. You can't trust them local witches. They're all out to get each other."

Before I could respond, Frank got back to the topic at hand. "Dave thinks the engine'll run, but he wants to change the oil and tune it up first. Your hull's a different story." He motioned to the waterline along the bottom of the boat.

"It's pocked out like crazy and needs some patching for sure. But you two can talk about his time schedule and cost. I've gotta get back to work on the other one, so I'll leave you both to it." Frank held up his coffee in thanks and headed down the wharf away from us. As he went, he murmured, "It'll be nice to have a decent cup of star anise again."

But I was stuck on the word cost. Hadn't he suggested his nephew might do it for free? If that wasn't the case, I planned to hire a professional. The time commitment comment also bothered me. How long might it take to get a professional down here to give me a quote? And would Frank be willing to oversee the work if I decided not to hire his nephew? Probably not.

I glanced at the date on my phone. It was already Sunday. How was I supposed to get all of this taken care of and get back by Tuesday?

Dave now lay flat on his back, half off the wharf, as though trying to see something along the lower half of my boat. "I thought I might be able to just paint over it and then give it a good wax, but that ain't gonna work."

"No? I'm really just looking for something fast and cheap, so I can get it up for sale."

Dave pushed up to his feet. He chewed a large wad of pink gum with an open mouth. "You ain't gonna get a good survey on it the way it is." He stared at me, waiting for a reply, but again, I felt out of my depth.

"Do I need one of those? A survey?" With houses, an inspection was usually required by mortgage companies, but I had no idea if this was the equivalent process with boats.

To this, he let out a loud guffaw. "Where do ya think you're gonna sell it?"

"Well, to be honest, I have no idea. But I have to take care of this quickly. And it sounds like you might not have the time, so—"

"Oh, I got the time. I just didn't know how much you wanted to spend, 'cause if you want it done right, I gotta rent a sander, and it'll need a couple coats of paint. We gotta ask Uncle Frank if we can dry-dock it up on shore for a couple days." He smack-smack-smacked his gum. "So I guess you gotta let me know about what you want."

I had to admit, the kid seemed to know a whole lot more about boats than I did. "How much do you think it might cost with the sander and the paint?"

He shrugged. "Probably quite a bit. Like five hundred. Or maybe seven."

Seven hundred dollars? Oh, what a sweet young boy. I'd spent seven hundred dollars on throw pillows once to sell a house. Even if it cost a thousand dollars to fix it up, I didn't think this was something I'd have to check over with my father.

"Okay, let's do it," I told Dave. "You're able to sand it yourself."

"Long as you get me a sander." He smacked his gum a few more times. "How 'bout I call in to see if I can rent one and then get started on the engine?"

Chapter Eleven

I DIDN'T KNOW HOW to judge competence when it came to mechanics, and yet two hours later when I heard the motor on the Lady of Fortune hum to life, I knew Frank was not exaggerating his nephew's abilities.

When he'd first come aboard the boat with me, Dave had helped me locate its registration papers in a cabinet under the dash in the little steering wheel section he called the cockpit. While he worked, I got busy online researching the make and model of the boat and digging into a few of the sales sites Dave had rattled off in passing. The boat might be worth more than I'd estimated but still far less than my dad had in mind. I also spent several hours scrubbing what Dave had called the "galley" but I just called it the miniature kitchen.

I ordered a pizza for us midafternoon, as I'd forgotten to pick up even a muffin at the café and my stomach was growling something awful.

Sherlock repeatedly rubbed up against my legs, and the questions Who's that? and Why's he here? kept rattling around in my mind. But I couldn't exactly answer him aloud while Dave was around.

"You wanna come look at this?" Dave never announced himself when he came into the cabin of the boat. He often stood there for who knew how long before he made a sound, and so far each time he'd done that had made me jump. But I was determined to get used to his silent lurking.

Once I calmed my racing heart, I stood up from my laptop. "Sure thing. What's up?"

The sun had set since I'd last heard word from him, and now he used a flashlight to lead me around to where the motor rested beneath the back of the boat.

He shone the flashlight at several different parts of the motor. "I was gonna clean it real good, but there's a lot of rust here, too. Usually, a clean motor helps with a quick sale, but I think here you'd be better to keep some of it covered up in grease. Ya think?"

When I'd bought my last car, even though it was an old model, the shiny engine was what sold me on it. But I had to admit, what Dave said made sense. Begrudgingly, I said, "Yeah, let's leave it."

He nodded and held up his phone. "I heard back from Happy Hardware. They got a sander put aside for you to pick up in the morning. It's fifty bucks a day."

I nodded and asked him for directions to Happy Hardware. It turned out it was just past The Heirloom Café, so maybe I'd get Frank and me another star anise coffee on my way.

"Do you drink coffee?" I asked Dave. "I'll pick you up something from the café in the morning, if you'd like."

"Nah, but I'd take a chocolate croissant if they got any. Usually, they're gone by ten."

I made a mental note and arranged to meet Dave back here the next day—Monday—which was the day I was hoping to head back to Portland. I supposed I'd have to call Brendan in the morning and try and buy myself at least another day.

Once Dave left, I slumped into the loveseat beside Sherlock, but before I could even put my feet up, a knock sounded at the door to the boat, making me jump once again.

"Come on in," I called, figuring Dave must have forgotten one of his tools. I hoped I hadn't locked it without thinking.

But the door swung open to reveal a pair of black-and-white striped tights. I followed them up to Rachael Adams's worried face. "You said I could drop by if I needed to talk?"

"Oh, sure, of course. Come on in." I pushed up straighter but didn't make a move to actually get up to meet her.

Rachael ducked to get through the door, even though she was quite short and her head didn't come anywhere near the top. I watched her as she proceeded to look around inside the boat, as though she was taking it all in with awe.

"You've never been aboard the Lady of Fortune?" I guessed. For once I had remembered to leave the words "my aunt" out of it.

"I have," she said pensively. As she moved inside, I had the immediate revelation of how strange it was that two spiritual people from this small town had died in such a short window of time. Of course, Aunt Lizzie's was a suicide, but still, I was thankful to see Rachael in one piece. The fact that I'd inadvertently encouraged her to go looking for Marigold's statue had been gnawing at me all afternoon.

While I had an automatic aversion to the crystal ball, Rachael seemed to have a magnetic pull toward it. A moment later, she sat almost in a trance at the small table. She didn't touch the crystal ball, but she ran a hand above it, as though feeling for any lasting heat.

It made me more than a little uncomfortable, especially with all I was still trying to process about Sherlock's strange mind-speak.

"Is this about your friend? Maple May?"

She nodded and looked at her lap. "I went to Marigold's house and looked for the statue. It wasn't on display anywhere, and I know she wouldn't hide it away. That would only decrease its power." I was stuck on the fact that it sounded as though Rachael had broken into her house when she asked, "What if Marigold really killed her?"

"Do you really think she's capable of something like that?" My mind ricocheted between the memory of the four of them trying to throw blame at one another and Dave's words about how he wouldn't trust a single one of them.

"Maybe not on her own. But what if Ruth helped her?"

"What would make you think either of them wanted to kill Maple May?"

Rachael reached for the crystal ball but again did not touch it. "Marigold was jealous of anyone who seemed like they were getting more attention than her for their magic. Maple May had started to gain a real following with the tourists, although that probably had more to do with her arrangement with one of the local tour guides." Now Rachael sounded slightly jealous herself.

I thought of the fact that Frank gave local tours. But from the sounds of things, he wasn't the only one. "And Ruth?" I asked.

Rachael pulled her hand from where it hovered near the crystal ball and took out her phone. It took her mere seconds to pull up a video and angle it my way.

I moved a couple of steps closer but kept my distance from the crystal ball. I felt extra nervous about it while there was a witch aboard the boat. I desperately wanted to get back to being the cynic I had been when I'd first come to town, but my mind wasn't letting that happen. In fact, if anything, the opposite was becoming true.

It was difficult to see what was on her phone, but it looked like two women arguing. Rachael turned up the volume, and then I could hear them better but still couldn't see them terribly well.

One said, "You've never belonged in this town and you know it! I suggest you find somewhere else to live or I'll make sure everyone at Witchy Wednesday knows where you came from and what you're hiding!"

"Go ahead and tell them anything you like," the other voice said, and the low tone of it was instantly familiar as Ruth, the potions specialist who I'd met at the café the day before. "You think anyone's going to take your word over mine?"

The argument went on, but Rachael clicked off her phone and laid it on the table. "See?"

The other woman must have been Maple May, but in truth, I couldn't tell if Ruth had taken Maple May's threat seriously. Then again, it was a threat. "Have you gone to the police with this information?" Regardless of what I—a visitor to this town—thought, if there truly was foul play involved in Maple May's death, Rachael should leave it in their hands to figure it out.

Besides, it would be nice to have the police's focus somewhere other than on me.

Her cheeks flushed a dark red. "I called Detective Jameson once. He's looking into the investigation."

"But did you show him that?" I motioned to her phone. Even though Rachael looked only a few years younger than me, she acted much younger.

She nibbled her lip. "He won't take it seriously. He'll just think I'm trying to throw blame. Besides, he's probably busy." As she said the words and blushed even harder, I saw the discomfort for what it really was: a schoolgirl crush.

Inwardly, I had to laugh. Who could blame her? Detective Jameson was attractive, there was no arguing that. But after he'd hidden his identity from me the way he had, I didn't feel any of the intimidation Rachael seemed to feel. In fact, I was looking for a reason to confront him about his underhandedness.

"Why would you think he wouldn't take the video seriously or wouldn't have time for it if it helps with an investigation?"

She shrugged. "It's from a long time ago. Before Christmas, and they'd been getting along ever since." Her eyes lingered on Sherlock. I wondered if, as a witch, she could tell there was something different about that cat.

I shook it off. "Still, it contains a clear threat. Would you like me to talk to the detective?" I had no idea why I kept offering advice and involving myself in this.

She looked up, meeting my eye. "Would you? And ask him if he can find out Ruth's last name. She won't tell any of us, and I'd really like to know what she's hiding." Her query sounded like it had more to do with personal reasons than the investigation.

Still, I shrugged with one shoulder. "I could at least find out where the investigation is at and suggest he contact you to see your video." I didn't particularly want her forwarding it to me. I already felt too close to this investigation. "Are the ladies from the Witchy Wednesday group truly so backbiting and jealous that they might have killed one of their own, though?"

"I wish I knew for sure." She sounded on the verge of tears, and she brought both hands within an inch of the crystal ball.

I tilted my head and motioned my chin toward it. "Is that telling you anything?"

When I'd first arrived, I hadn't put any stock in the thing, but now I held my breath, as my stance had clearly changed on all things supernatural.

She squeezed her eyes shut but, a few seconds later, let out a huff of a sigh and dropped her hands to her lap. "Despite coming from a long line of witches, I don't do well with magic. I'm still trying to find my way."

"Your mom's a witch?" I raised my eyebrows.

"And my grandmother. And my great-grandmother. Your Aunt Lizzie had offered to help me, but just my luck, she died before we could even get started. No one else in this town seems to want to help anyone else." She glanced again at Sherlock.

So she hadn't missed me mentioning my relationship to my aunt. "Maple May didn't want to help you?" I asked, quickly changing the subject.

Rachael sighed. "She tried. But it always went horribly wrong. One time I tried to cast a spell to help me find a new place to live because I didn't like the smell of smoke from my landlords. Their place caught on fire that same afternoon. All my stuff was ruined and then they kicked me out. Another time, I tried a potion from Ruth that was supposed to make my hair grow. It turned green, and I had to cut it all off.

Although, I'm still not sure that she didn't sell me the wrong potion on purpose."

Whoa, those really were a group of backbiting witches.

But I had to admit, I found them interesting, if nothing else. If I got to know Rachael a little bit better, I might even feel like I could ask her about the strange things I was experiencing since being in Crystal Cove. And I wasn't terribly disappointed about having a reason to call Detective Jay Jameson.

"Tell me more about Maple May. How long did you know her? Did she have family here in Crystal Cove?"

"I think her family's still in Portland," Rachael said. "She didn't get along with them and came down here to get away from their pressure."

"Pressure?" I suddenly wondered if she had family who would have been angry enough with Maple May to want to hurt her.

Rachael shrugged. "She used to be Miss Oregon. She said her mother always lived vicariously through her, and she moved here a few years ago to try out the small-town life instead."

Even after her death, I'd been able to tell Maple May had been attractive, but a beauty queen? That seemed to give a whole new set of reasons for jealousy. But I reminded myself this was not my case to solve. I wasn't even from here and I'd never met the girl, for heaven's sake.

"Hey, my dad asked me to quickly sell this boat and keep quiet that Lizzie was my aunt. Would you mind not mentioning it to anyone?"

She looked at me for a long moment before nodding. I hoped it didn't mean she'd already told people. I also hoped she wouldn't ask me why my dad asked for that.

Finally, she said, "I'm pretty good at keeping secrets. Just let me know what Detective Jameson says."

Chapter Twelve

EARLY THE NEXT DAY, I headed up to Happy Hardware and grabbed the sander that had been reserved for me. I'd brought my car, not knowing how large this sander might be, but it turned out I could have easily walked with it.

On my way back, I stopped in for three chocolate croissants and two star anise brews.

None of the witches seemed to be around this early, but half of the rest of the town was here, forming a lineup almost to the door. Two ladies ahead of me immediately turned around when I joined the line.

"You're not from around here." The lady's blunt statement took me aback. She was in her sixties, with white hair and a tense expression. I felt as though I should retreat right back out the door.

But another one of my dad's campaigning mottos was that you could turn anyone to your side with enough charm and compassion. Strange, now that I thought about it, those two words coming out of my father's mouth.

In his case, it was clearly an act, but I took a breath, donned my most genuine smile, and said, "Boy, Avrum wasn't kidding when he said everyone knew everyone in this small town."

I caught Avrum's eye, and hearing his name, he lifted a hand in a wave to me. The sixtysomething woman followed my gaze and offered her own wave to Avrum. When she turned back to me, she was smiling.

I remembered another one of my dad's mantras: sometimes all it takes is having the right friends.

"What brings you to Crystal Cove, dear?"

"Sadly, I'm only here for a few days. Just long enough to fix up a boat and get it up for sale."

"A boat?" the other lady asked. She was about the same age but looked younger with dyed blonde hair. "Which one?"

"The Lady of Fortune." I tried to say the words casually, but the white-haired lady gasped and slapped a hand over her mouth.

A man, who had joined the line behind me, asked, "Are you Lizzie's niece, then?"

I thought Rachael said she could keep a secret. Before I could turn and come up with an answer, the white-haired lady grasped one of my hands. "Just awful what happened to your aunt."

With her statement, this idea hit me anew, and this time it made me angry: nothing had happened to Aunt Lizzie. She'd done it by her own hand. It wasn't like with that witch Maple May. Whatever had happened to her clearly was not her fault.

The others in the lineup took my pause as grief-stricken. The blonde woman rested a hand on my shoulder. I wasn't used to being touched, especially by strangers. The line had moved forward, so it gave me a reason to motion ahead to them.

Thankfully, they both dropped their hands to move forward.

The man behind me was the next to speak. He was tall—well over six feet—but seemed to be trying to show his compassion by hunching forward. "I'm afraid you've caught Crystal Cove at a bad time. Sadly, we've had another death in our midst, just this last weekend."

"That's awful," I said, as though I knew nothing about it, but mostly I was just thankful for the subject change and that word of me being first on the scene hadn't traveled as fast. "Did any of you know her?"

"Well, of course," the white-haired lady said. Her tone had gone tense again. "Everybody knew Maple May, but if you ask me, somebody ran her over on purpose."

"She was hit by a car?" I asked, figuring maybe word on the street was a viable way to figure out where an investigation was at in a town as small as this one.

"Now, now," the man behind me said. "We don't know that it was intentional."

"We don't know that it wasn't," the blonde lady said. She'd adopted a biting tone as well.

The line moved forward again, and it was the blonde lady's turn to order. She whipped around to face Avrum, who greeted her with a gruff, "What can I get you, Mabel?"

I was surprised at Avrum's tone, but then when he moved to the rear counter to make up Mabel's Earl Grey tea, I noticed him rubbing his temples.

He was no more pleasant when he served the white-haired lady, a woman he called, "Tracy."

Before the ladies left to find a table with their large mugs, Mabel turned back to me. "We hope you have a nice stay in Crystal Cove, regardless, Tabitha."

This time I was sure I hadn't told them my own name, but as if to somehow grab some footing in this conversation, I called out, "Thanks, Mabel!" as though I knew them just as well as they knew me.

"What can I get you, Tabitha?" Avrum's grumbly tone hadn't improved any.

I leaned a little closer and said, "You should really try some mint on your temples." I glanced at the stalks of lavender, which he seemed to have forgotten about as well.

But he just cleared his throat in annoyance, so I put in my order, and Dave had been right—I'd ended up getting the last three croissants.

I returned to the marina feeling a mix of regret and comfort. The inhabitants of a town selling the supernatural were a lot more normal than I expected. Sure, they liked to gossip, but they also had time in their day to notice and care about things that happened.

I was supposed to keep my relation to Aunt Lizzie quiet, but that seemed impossible in a town this size. And was that really such a bad thing? Even though I would never want to be struck down by a car to my death or whatever had happened to Maple May, I'd like to know there'd at least be some people who would notice and care if it did happen.

I called out for Frank on my way down the wharf, but he was nowhere in sight. I carried the sander and my coffee tray with the croissant bag stacked on top around the corner toward my boat and was surprised to see Dave already there. He appeared to be pacing.

"Oh, good. Finally," he said when he saw me.

"I got there as soon as the hardware store opened at nine," I told him.

He stopped pacing and helped himself to a croissant when I held out the bag toward him. "I just figured I could get to work on fixing that oil leak before sanding but then realized you'd left the boat locked."

I already had my set of keys in my hand. Had he really expected me to just leave it open? My parents had passed along two keys, and they were both the same, as there was only one door to get inside the houseboat. I hesitated for a second, then decided I trusted Dave. After all, he was helping me for just the cost of supplies. I looked from the door to the cabin and back to the front deck, where Sherlock sat up at attention on one of the wrought iron chairs, watching my every move.

Whenever I got away from the boat for any amount of time, I tended to forget about the oddities I'd experienced since being here—especially, the oddities concerning that cat. Each time I returned, I took one look at him and felt like I was going crazy all over again. Surely I hadn't been hearing him talking to me. Right?

He wriggled his nose to push his glasses up as if he could hear me thinking about him.

Finally, I shook off my confusion, pulled a copy of the boat key off the ring, and passed it over to Dave. "Why don't you take this? Just in case I'm not here whenever you come here to work.

Which reminds me . . . how long do you expect it to take to fix this thing up?"

He shrugged. "A week or two, if I work at it every day." He went on, but I got lost in my own thoughts. I'd been putting off asking because deep down I knew Tuesday was fast approaching and I'd have to call Brendan today. "Uncle Frank said we could dry-dock it if we got it out before he leaves on his tour, but it's gonna take me at least a couple days just to sand the hull. Then it needs filling and painting."

"And do you need me here for that?" I asked, still trying to find a way to not have to confront my boss.

He shrugged. "Guess not, but if I find anything else that needs fixin', it'd sure be nice to be able to ask you what you want done."

Hmm. I could call my dad and ask what he thought about all this, but I already knew his answer. He'd want me to stick around and get it done. I had been determined to keep my job with Reiger Realty without a word from our state senator to pave my way, but I suddenly wondered if that was going to be possible. Besides, it wasn't as if it was my fault I was stuck here.

Before I made a decision, another figure made his way down the dock. Even from a distance, I could see those eyelashes. I'd put it out of my mind that I'd left a message for Detective Jameson to call me back when he had a minute. Apparently, he had more than a minute. He had long enough to stop by in person, which only made my heart flutter harder.

I held the coffee tray out toward Dave, trying to ignore the detective and catch my breath. "If you see your uncle, can you give him his coffee? And there's an extra croissant here for you." Even though my mouth had been watering earlier when I smelled them in the café, I suddenly couldn't see myself stomaching anything.

I took one last deep breath and then walked toward the detective and met him halfway down the dock. "You got my message." My voice was curt.

He nodded once. Unlike the other day, when he'd been here in jeans, today he wore a suit, and his serious expression made him look every part the detective. "Can we go inside and talk?" He motioned to the Lady of Fortune where Dave now sat cross-legged on the dock, looking over the sander like a kid with a new toy.

I crossed my arms. "First, I'd love to know why you hid your identity from me the last time you were here."

His eyebrows shot up, which made him look attractive in more of a boyish way. "Hid? I didn't hide anything. You didn't ask."

I scowled. "Right, because I ask everyone who drops by if they happen to be a detective."

"Look, Tabby . . ." I hated to admit it, even to myself, but his use of my nickname and the fact that he even remembered it softened me. "I understand why you might feel tricked, but please understand my point of view. It's my job to investigate, and in this case, I'm investigating a possible homicide. Sometimes I have to keep a few things up my sleeve in order to get to the truth."

A few things up his sleeve? Was that what he called it? But it made sense, as much as I hated to admit it. And if I could help him get to the truth, I wanted to do that.

He offered a small smile, which disarmed the rest of me that had yet to relax. "Can we move past this, Tabby? Forgive and forget?" He tilted his head, as though it took work to see past those eyelashes. "Let's go inside and talk."

I wasn't sure how soundproof the boat was, nor was I completely sure I wanted Detective Jameson snooping around my aunt's boat. The last time he'd been here, it had been to investigate me without me even knowing he was doing it. But when he started walking toward it without my permission, I decided I had nothing to hide. In fact, I hoped my forthrightness would help them solve this investigation. If I couldn't have as quick success with selling my aunt's boat as I had hoped, at least I could go home knowing I'd done something important here.

I opened the door to the cabin and let him go in first. While I had a paranoia about my aunt's crystal ball and Rachael had had what seemed like a healthy fear of it, Detective Jameson strode straight for it and actually picked it up from its stand.

I stopped in place, stunned and at least half worried that the sky might implode onto the boat.

"What can you tell us about what happened, huh?"

In my stunned state, I thought he was asking me. I opened my mouth to answer, but before I could get a word out, he turned the ball in his hands, tilted his head, and peered closer into it. As he did this, it gave off a pinkish glow. I pulled back, wondering if there was some kind of pressure sensor inside the ball. But at the same time, I worried it might be more than that.

I swallowed. "Do you know how to work one of those?"

He looked back at me. "No. Do you?"

I shook my head. "But I mean, if you don't know how to work it, don't you think you should put it down?" The longer he held it, and the longer I was on my aunt's boat, the more I believed it had more than just a pressure sensor. Much more. And people who didn't know what they were doing probably shouldn't play around with it.

He turned it over a few more times in his hands and then placed it back onto its wooden stand. He didn't take his hands away for several long seconds and kept peering into it.

"You don't see anything, right?" I guessed.

A mix of relief and disappointment washed over me when he shook his head. "But your aunt sure could see a lot in it."

"Can you just keep it down about that?" I whispered, not wanting Dave to hear. Then again, it seemed like most of the town already knew Lizzie was my aunt.

A low meow caught my attention. I looked over to see Sherlock curled up on the loveseat. I did a double take. The cat hadn't come in with us, so how had he gotten inside? I shook my head at the thoughts that were trying to make their way into my head and told myself there had to be some kind of doggie door I'd been missing.

Regardless of how he got in, he couldn't possibly be sleeping already. I had barely known the cat for a couple of days, but I already knew him well enough to recognize his ears pricked up, as if he was listening carefully to our every word.

"Keep it down about what?" Detective Jameson asked, looking around the empty boat cabin.

"Look, I came to town to sell the boat, hopefully quietly. Because of the way my aunt died, my family doesn't want to bring attention to her connection with us."

Detective Jameson tilted his head at me. His eyes widened when the truth of it seemed to settle him. "You're from that Chase family?"

"Shhh!" I told him again, this time more vehemently. Even though my first name had made the local rounds, I didn't think my last name had. Yet.

He furrowed his brow, taking this in. "But yet you called to talk about a local murder investigation?"

"It was declared a murder then?" I asked. "You know that for sure?"

Detective Jameson sighed and pulled out a chair from the table to take a seat. "The medical examiner found a narrow contusion to her skull, which doesn't line up with injuries she would have sustained as a pedestrian being struck with a car. She appeared to have died from one solid hit." When he spoke, his words were much more formal and precise than the first time I'd met him.

"Narrow contusion? So she was hit with something on the head?"

He nodded. "All signs lead to that, yes. Now, you said you had some information pertaining to the case?"

"Well, not me so much as Rachael Adams, the local witch." When he showed recognition of the name, I went on. "She believes there are members of her Witchy Wednesday group who would have wanted to kill Maple May."

His forehead buckled again. "And why wouldn't Miss Adams have told me this directly?"

I didn't want to mention her crush if I didn't have to. "I think she was uncomfortable because she sees all these ladies regularly. I said I had to contact you anyway, and I'm sure she'd be happy to answer any further questions you have for her."

"Okay." He raised his eyebrows at me. "So who does she think did it?" He sat back in his seat.

"She has an older video clip you might find interesting. It included Ruth threatening Maple May. Rachael thinks several of the witches within the Witchy Wednesday group had motivation or at least had jealous feelings toward Maple May, but she thinks it was either Marigold Weathers or Ruth . . . I don't know her last name—or perhaps they were in it together. Can you find out anything about Ruth's last name or her past?"

Detective Jameson pulled a notebook from his suit jacket pocket and made a note. "I'm afraid there are too many people in town who were jealous of Maple May to list." I thought again of Mabel and Tracy at the café, who had immediately taken on a tension when Maple May was mentioned. "Because of the way the body was placed—and not dragged—we figured it must have been someone strong. Plus, it's not easy to make a clean break at the knee like that. It would probably have to be someone stronger than these ladies you're suggesting. But we hadn't yet considered a collaboration . . ."

"Marigold Weathers looks quite strong." Ruth, on the other hand, did not. "Who else have you considered?"

He shook his head. "I'm afraid I can't tell you that, but if you—or Rachael," he said as though I may have only been using Rachael's name as a front to get involved, "come up with any other ideas, I'd love to hear them. We've considered the Witches' group, of course, but we're also interested to hear of others in town who may have held some sort of grudge toward the victim. If Rachael has any ideas about anyone like that, do let me know."

I didn't appreciate his tone, but I told him about Mabel and Tracy at the café, regardless. He showed recognition and marked their names down, but I didn't get the sense he thought much of them as suspects. In truth, neither of them looked strong enough for what he was suggesting.

"I'll be sure to ask Rachael the next time I see her as well." I crossed my arms.

He looked like he was barely paying attention to me, though. Instead, his eyes scanned the interior of the boat. On a whim, I thought I'd try a new tactic to help me clear out this boat. "You said you might be interested in purchasing some of Lizzie's furnishings. Or was that only a ploy to get me talking about the investigation?"

The detective looked slightly sheepish when he said, "No, I really would purchase some if they're for sale."

"I might be willing to part with some of them if you tell me why you're interested."

Detective Jameson shrugged, still looking sheepish or maybe just sad. "Your aunt used to be one of my informants."

"Lizzie was really an informant for the police?" I whispered back.

He nodded solemnly, and in that moment, I knew he had liked my aunt. In turn, I felt myself warm to him. "We had many conversations on this boat. With the Lady of Fortune still docked here, it almost still feels like there's a piece of her left in Crystal Cove. I have to admit, I'll be sad to see the boat go."

"Were you friends with Aunt Lizzie, then?" I felt like a little kid asking this. He'd just said she had been an informant, but I couldn't help myself.

He nodded. "You could definitely say that. I was shocked and saddened when I heard about her death. I had known she had some stresses, and she had seemed sad the last time I spoke with her, but I hadn't realized she was suicidal."

"And you're sure her death couldn't have been the result of another jealous witch in town?"

Before he even shook his head and gave his response, I knew the answer. As difficult as it had been to hear the details of it all, my mom still had Lizzie's suicide note. It was in her own loopy handwriting and had contained her ever-present note of hope—talking about flying off the cliff into the great beyond.

"With her suicide note and her sister's identification, we were certain her death was by her own hand."

I couldn't let myself dwell on this. It was too hard to think about. "What sorts of things did Lizzie inform you on for your investigations?" I was truly interested. And I had to wonder if Lizzie was the one giving the police information or she'd had some strange magical thing going on with her cat as well.

As if the cat could feel me wondering about him, he opened an eye in what looked like a reverse wink. It made his eyeglasses sit funny. Detective Jameson turned to see what I was looking at, but Sherlock quickly closed both eyes.

"She would often tell me if we were on the right track. Sometimes it took her a day or two of consulting her wares . . ." He ran a hand over the crystal ball, and again a pink hue filled it, but nothing else appeared. "While my partners in forensics were busy studying all the cold hard evidence, I always checked in with Lizzie. She could quickly sort through the evidence we had uncovered and tell us what was most important. Sometimes she could even lead us toward a suspect we hadn't considered." He pulled his hand away from the crystal ball and shook his head. "To be honest, she was an integral part of our team. I wonder how many crimes will go unsolved without her around to help us."

"And you can't go get help from any of the other witches in town?"

He looked at the table and twisted his lips. A long moment passed before he looked up and said, "I'm not one to challenge anyone's abilities, but I've just never seen verified evidence from anyone else that they have a strong enough skill set in this area. And believe me, I've tried."

Him saying this made me wonder why the witches would choose to kill Maple May over their jealous feelings if they hadn't killed Aunt Lizzie.

By the time the detective got up to leave, I had a strong feeling there was someone the police and Rachael were overlooking.

I looked over at the sleeping cat and wondered if he had been the one sorting through the evidence. And if he'd done it once, could he do it again?

Chapter Thirteen

MREAOW!

I had barely shut the door behind Detective Jameson when Sherlock made it clear he was wide awake.

"Do you recognize that detective?" As stupid as I felt talking to the cat out loud, I had to get a handle on just how much Sherlock tuned into human relationships and if he indeed was trying to communicate with me. Especially if he had been the true police informant.

He jumped from the loveseat and arched his back high in a stretch. I tried to read into this but came up with nothing.

Then he paced to what I was learning to call the galley. He popped up on his hind legs to get both front paws behind the cupboard that housed his food. A long fumbly minute later, he had his food container open and tipped onto its side with his head in the opening.

"Do you want me to put that in a bowl for you?" I asked.

At this, he pulled his head out of the container, sat back on his haunches, and looked up at me.

I took the empty porcelain cat bowl from the floor and gave it a quick wash. When I returned with it, Sherlock was still sitting on his haunches waiting for me. As I poured his food into his bowl, I decided to try again. "That detective? Had you ever seen him here with Lizzie?"

He took a bite and chewed through several mouthfuls before a phrase came into my head that I was pretty sure hadn't come from me.

Do you think he was lying?

"I don't know. What do you think?" That cat was the intuitive one, after all.

Sherlock took another bite and chewed. I wondered if eating helped him think. I did not get the sense he was the lying type.

I decided even if this was just me sorting through my subconscious thoughts, it was a good, positive move. Because of the political world I'd grown up in, I tended to think the worst of people. While I easily recognized the shifty ones, I didn't always trust my ability to read the good ones—especially when it came to attractive men, apparently. Being in this strange town, it was nice to know there were people—or at least felines—I could trust.

"Do you think he has any magical abilities?" I asked.

Another bite. He seemed more like he hoped you could help him in that way. Sherlock let out a sound, which at first I thought was him choking on his kibble, but when I looked down at him and he met my gaze with a Cheshire-cat-type smile, I realized it was actually a chuckle.

He wasn't wrong. Me having magical abilities was a ridiculous notion.

To get us back on track, I figured why not ask the obvious question. "Did anything Detective Jameson said give you a sense of who killed the dead witch, Maple May Doerksen?"

Sherlock wiggled his nose to push his glasses back up into place. No, but then again, I didn't know the woman, so it's hard to have any sense.

At the very least, I was getting more comfortable conversing with the cat. Whether or not that was a good thing or simply a sign of my mental instability, I wasn't completely sure. "What if you had someone to tell you more about the woman?" I thought of having Rachael back over here, and again as if Sherlock could read my thoughts, a new thought came into my head.

That striped-legged witch has some answers.

"Rachael? Do you think she was lying? Do you think she could have killed Maple May?" I wondered again if he might have been communicating with her while she was aboard the boat as well.

But Sherlock tilted his head. Took another bite. Chewed. If you want to solve this mystery, she's our best lead.

"So that's our next move? To get Rachael back over here?" I shook off that thought quickly. Why was I so concerned about getting myself involved in this murder investigation anyway? I should let the police do their job.

Sherlock lifted a front paw and licked it. I can't tell you if someone is trustworthy until I can see them with my own two eyes.

With his own two eyes only with his glasses on, I reminded myself. I wondered if I attached more blue crystals to that cat, could he give me all the answers to the universe?

And if so, where on earth could I find more crystals?

Chapter Fourteen

AS IT TURNED OUT, I didn't get around to finding Rachael and inviting her back to the boat before we had another unexpected visitor. I almost didn't recognize the detective when I opened the door to the cabin to his knock, and all I could chalk that up to was the smile on his face.

"Hi, Miss Chase. Do you have a minute to talk?"

Last I saw him, it had been dark and miserable out, to match his personality, so maybe I should have expected his countenance to brighten with the skies.

But I had to blink twice before his name actually came to me.

"Detective Thom?" I looked up and down the dock. I wasn't sure why. Maybe to see if there was someone else he might be smiling at, but even Dave had run off to grab some tools from home, so we were alone. "Your partner was by about an hour ago to talk to me."

Even with his current smile, I felt a lot more eager to have Detective Jameson inside the houseboat than this hot and cold guy.

He furrowed his brow. "My partner?"

"Detective Jameson." I said his name slowly, with a sudden sick feeling coming over me. What if Detective Jameson had only been pretending to be a detective? What if I'd had him pegged right in the first place and he was only one of those eager mystical types who wanted to trick me into getting rid of anything that might lead him to higher enlightenment?

I had to know at least what I was working with here. "Yeah, tall blond guy? I think he said his name was Jameson . . ." I pretended to search for more and soon it worked. Detective Thom filled in the blank.

"Detective Jay Jameson?" When I nodded, he said, "Oh, we're on the same force, but we're not partners. I just call him in on certain cases when one of his . . . specialties is needed."

"Specialties?" I asked. I still hadn't invited him inside.

Detective Thom shrugged. "I'm a forensics expert. I study the science of a crime scene. Jameson's better with . . ." He searched for the word for several long seconds, shifting on his feet and looking more and more uncomfortable.

"Otherworldly stuff?" I guessed.

"So you have met him." He chuckled at his own little joke, but I wasn't so easily charmed. I still worried that this was all a ploy to get me to let my guard down and suddenly he'd become the ogre I'd met on the roadside the other night. "Jameson was telling me about the wares your aunt has on her boat here, and I'm looking to match up something specific."

If you'd told me a week ago that I'd meet two good-looking detectives—now that he wore a smile, I had to admit to Detective Thom's attractiveness—and that I'd feel more at ease with the one preoccupied with the mystical than the one with a head for science, I'd have said you were crazy. With this revelation, I decided on the spot that we'd simply gotten off on the wrong foot, when he'd been stressed about a recent death under his jurisdiction. Who wouldn't be stressed about something like that?

I was about to paste on my own smile and invite him inside when he pulled something out of his pocket and held it out to show me. It was the exact same type of blue jewel I'd found the other night on the roadside.

I swallowed. "What's that?"

"As far as I can tell, it's a blue crystal. We found two of them at the scene of our investigation the other night. Jameson suspects they're used in some kind of sorcery, so I just wanted to stop by and see if you've come across anything like this on your aunt's boat."

I pulled the door an inch shut behind me. Last I'd seen him, Sherlock had been curled up on the loveseat. I knew exactly where two more of those crystals were, but my aunt clearly wasn't a suspect, as she'd already been dead when Maple May was killed. Because I probably shouldn't have taken something from the crime scene and I was already a suspect, though, what good would it do to admit as much?

At least that was what I told myself as I reached for the crystal, pretending to want to have a closer look at it.

"It's pretty. And it's a crystal, you say?" I hoped the awe to my voice would be enough so he didn't ask me again.

But the second I had it in my hand, that voice, the one I could swear came from my aunt's cat, came through so loud and clear, I was sure Detective Thom would be able to hear it, too. *Pretty crystal? Where's the pretty crystal? Is it blue?*

I kept my gaze fixed on the crystal as Detective Thom asked, "You haven't by chance seen anything like one of these around your aunt's boat?" His voice was so calm and even, he couldn't have heard Sherlock.

But the cat was again loud and clear when he added, Tell him you're busy packing. If there's any other crystals among Lizzie's stuff, you'll let him know right away.

I repeated the words almost verbatim and pasted on my best politician's smile. But then as another image came into my head again, I had the urge to tell him about that, too, even if I didn't know if there was any real truth to it.

"Did you check the scene of the investigation for a hair comb? I thought I saw one on the woman on the road, and it might have had some of these jewels in it." As I spoke the words, I became less convinced. It had only been a dream, and what if I was wasting this detective's time?

Although, better that than have him searching my aunt's boat and her cat for the crystals.

"And you say the victim was wearing this comb when you found her?" His smile faded. This was definitely new information to him, so I suspected they had not found a comb on Maple May.

In my dream, she'd been wearing the comb—but she'd also been alive. I shook my head. "Honestly, that night was such a blur. I'm not sure what I saw and where. It was all so shocking. This crystal, it just looks familiar, and I thought it might be from a comb I'd seen."

Detective Thom tilted his head, and I could sense he was about to grill me more about when, exactly, I'd seen this and what the comb had looked like, but then Sherlock's voice came through loud and clear again, giving me another idea.

If Maple May had crystals on the road, there has to be more. What about at her house? What about her family?

"Have you spoken to Maple May's family?" I blurted before he could ask anything else about the comb. "Or searched her house for more of these blue crystals?"

Detective Thom looked down for a long moment, as though offering a moment of silence for Maple May's grieving family. "Her sister came into town to identify her body, and she's staying in town to pack up Maple May's apartment."

"Not her parents?" I asked, recalling what Rachael had said about how Maple May had escaped the pressure from her mom by coming to Crystal Cove.

Detective Thom furrowed his brow. "We've been in touch with them, but it seems they're having some trouble processing their grief. We were glad Sonya Doerksen was willing to drive into town to help us with the postmortem details." Detective Thom held out his hand for me to pass the crystal back. I didn't want to. I'd never heard the cat-thoughts so clearly and from such a distance, and he'd never been quite this helpful. But as the detective waited with his hand outstretched, I had no choice.

"You said you found two of these?" I asked.

Detective Thom nodded. "They were several feet from the victim's body, so they may be unrelated, but at this point, we're following all leads."

I wondered what Sonya Doerksen—the sister of a beauty queen—was like. Had she been a jealous sister? Was she a witch? And had she found any blue crystals, or maybe a comb, while cleaning up her sister's apartment? I knew I should leave this to the police, and yet, if Maple May owned a comb with blue crystals in it, and it hadn't been at the scene of her death, how would I explain that?

I reminded myself that it had only been a dream. But before I'd even processed that thought, I knew I didn't really believe it. There was something more happening to me in Crystal Cove, and it wasn't only about this town. It was about this boat. It definitely had to do with my aunt's spectacled cat. And probably the blue crystals.

"Maybe you should check with some of the other witches in town," I suggested. "They probably have a better idea of where to find more crystals and what they're used for."

"That's a good idea," he said, placing the crystal back into a baggie and then into his pocket. "I'll certainly follow up with them." He handed me another of his business cards. "Do call me if you find anything interesting around your aunt's boat, though, would you?"

I still couldn't get over how friendly he seemed compared to the other night. And the more I looked at him, the more attractive he became. His angular cheekbones and dark hair, along with his dark blue eyes, gave him a compelling look and I didn't want to turn away. "You bet."

"How long did you say you'd be in town?"

I'd been trying my best to get out of town as quickly as possible, but the thought of leaving with so many unanswered questions plaguing me—not to mention a talking cat—suddenly had me looking for reasons to stay. "This boat's going to take longer to fix up than I anticipated. I should probably be around for at least a few more days."

"Oh, good. Do you have time for dinner, then?"

My mouth went dry. Was he asking me out? "Um . . ."

"You have to eat, right? How about tomorrow night?" There was a bit of an edge to his voice, as if he was suddenly nervous or bracing for my rejection.

His good looks aside, I wanted to do it, if nothing else to hear more about the case. I nodded hesitantly. I didn't know exactly how to pry yet, but who else could tell me more about the truth behind these blue crystals than a forensics expert?

Chapter Fifteen

"WHAT IS IT WITH those crystals?" I asked myself the moment Detective Thom disappeared down the dock. I made my way into the boat cabin as I thought it over. They couldn't just be about a communicative cat, could they? And why would the detective have come here to see if I knew anything about them?

Maybe they think you have special powers, like Lizzie. Maybe they thought you placed the crystals at the scene of the crime and cast a spell.

This made me laugh. Sherlock looked up at me from the loveseat, as if waiting for my answer. But what if my dreams did mean something? What if this magic I was experiencing was no joke?

Still, I was quite sure I hadn't cast a spell on Maple May that had brought her death. When I glanced over, Sherlock had moved from the loveseat to the full box of detective novels. He pawed over them, sniffing at each one.

"Is there an answer in one of those?" I asked.

He didn't look up or stop sniffing. Remembering the way he'd pawed through a book the other night, I figured it couldn't hurt to help him out, even if it undid some of my packing.

I placed him aside for a moment and pulled the novels out one by one, placing them on the floor of the boat. Sherlock continued sniffing and opening books, but as he quickly moved from one to another, I could tell he wasn't finding anything noteworthy.

I sat back and surveyed the boat, which still needed a ton of work on both the inside and the outside. It was already Monday, and I'd gone ahead and made a dinner appointment—a date—for tomorrow night, so the next item I had on my agenda was either calling my dad or calling my boss.

I chose my dad first, not because he was any less threatening or easier to talk to, but I wondered if I could somehow get him to work his senator magic on my boss.

My dad answered his cell on the fourth ring, which meant he was busy, and the sounds of his office filled the background. "How's the boat coming, Tabitha? Tell me you have good news."

"I do," I offered in my brightest tone. "As I said, it needs a lot of work, but I've found a local mechanic who offered to do a lot of the work for just the cost of supplies."

A pause and then, "Why would he do that?"

Right. I should have prepared my words a little better and known Dad would be suspicious of every little bit of small-town kindness. "Oh, he's the nephew of the man who owns the marina here. He's in school and needed a project to do for his practicum." I hoped phrasing it this way would make my dad assume it was some kind of trade school the way I had.

"Did you write up a contract for him?"

The one part about real estate that my dad had complimented me on again and again was my adeptness with learning how to draft contracts. I didn't want to lie to him, and yet I found myself saying, "Yes, Dad, but I wanted to talk to you about the timeline."

He sounded distracted, talking to someone in the background for a minute, and then said, "What's that, Tab?"

"The mechanic said it'll take a few days to sand the rust off the hull and paint it, so I guess I'm stuck here."

"Okay, great, great. And then you'll get it listed?" He was still distracted.

"Well, that's the thing. I'm concerned about my job at Reiger Realty."

"You'll work it out. Hey, I told you not to print those!" It took me a second to realize he wasn't talking to me.

He was clearly too busy to focus and he wasn't going to help me keep my job. But was that what I wanted, anyway? The reason I'd gotten the job in the first place was to prove myself to him.

So I let my dad get back to whatever political fire he had to put out, hung up, and then picked up the phone again to call Brendan.

Chapter Sixteen

IT TOOK ME TEN minutes of waiting on hold to finally get Brendan on the line.

"Oh, good, you're back," he said. "Get down to the office. I have a list of things I need done, and—"

"I'm still in Crystal Cove," I blurted, cutting him off.

A pause followed, and I felt his anger and frustration before he even spoke again. "You're . . . where?"

I had to cut it off and deal with this professionally. "I realize I'll have to use up my holiday time on this, and I've never taken a sick day, so I'm happy to use those if need be, but I need a few—"

"What? You're not back?" He wouldn't let me get a word in edgewise. "I was depending on you to help set up tomorrow, to draft up contracts for the Roseland apartments, to—"

I wondered suddenly if I could do some of that remotely. Not set up for open houses, of course, but the contracts and any research that needed to be done. But I opened my mouth and started with, "I can—"

He cut me off to say, "You're fired! Don't come back for a month, for all I care. I'll hire someone I can depend on."

I'd never been fired before. Sure, I'd given up on numerous jobs or careers over the years, but no one had ever said the words, "You're fired."

After he hung up on me, I sat at my aunt's table, stunned, for several long seconds. Even if this wasn't my fault, it hit me hard between the teeth. How would I admit to my dad that I couldn't figure it out? Of course Dad had never thought as much of Reiger Realty as I had. He had never seemed to even notice whether or not I had potential as a realtor.

I had been determined to make this career work. To show him, to show all the classmates I'd grown up with, that I could be someone successful. I'd wanted to establish myself by our ten-year high school reunion. I'd distanced myself from most of my longtime friends over the years, claiming busyness, but now with the reunion only three months away, it was the worst possible time to find myself unemployed.

Even Sherlock seemed to know I wouldn't be good company tonight and stayed away from the boat. I'd finally located his cat door—under a curtain near the front of the cabin, and I had to admit, it brought me great relief to know he wasn't blinking his eyes and muttering a magic spell to get in and out. But I looked in that direction and the curtain didn't move.

I sighed. I had to get out of here and find something to eat. I'd barely made my way to Main Street when I decided now that I was out of a job, I'd better watch my pennies. I'd seen a grocery mart on the corner near the café, and I headed there in search of something cheap I could cook, provided I could get my aunt's hot plate working.

I'd been wanting to keep my bad mood to myself, but imagine my surprise when I opened the door to the grocery mart and recognized the purple hair behind the register.

Marigold Weathers was a grocery clerk?

That was surprising, to say the least. She looked much different today in plain black slacks, a white blouse, and a green apron over top. She was with a customer and didn't see me at first, so I slipped down the first aisle to get out of sight. Moving along the rear of the store, I padded down the last aisle, which would put me closer to the till but still out of sight.

"You have a nice night now, Mrs. Granger. And do come and see me on the weekend if you need any further direction. I'll give you your next reading for half price!" Marigold's voice sounded even peppier than it had when she'd been telling me about Witchy Wednesday.

It was silent after that, short of the elevator music playing through the speakers in the ceiling. I no longer cared much about what I would eat. I was eager to put thoughts of Reiger Realty behind me and talk to Marigold.

I grabbed a package of basmati rice from the shelf beside me and a packet of Thai spice paste and headed for the counter.

Marigold did a double take when she recognized me. "Oh! You're still in town?" I couldn't detect if it was suspicion or interest that lay behind her words.

I nodded. "The boat is going to take longer than I expected to fix up. Plus, I no longer have to race back to Portland."

"No? Why's that?" She rang up my two items and gave me the total.

I shrugged, then figured maybe it was better to admit the truth to someone else before I had to say it to my father. "I was delayed, and so my boss fired me."

Her eyebrows shot up as she passed me my change and placed my items in a bag. "What will you do now?"

I looked toward the door and, beyond that, the marina. "I have no idea."

Even as I admitted this, I didn't feel as worried as I probably should have. There was something about this town and that boat—not to mention that cat—that made me feel surprisingly calm about the chaos that had come into my life in the past few days.

"Well, dear, you should definitely come and see me on the weekend. We'll get your future sorted out. And since you're going to be in town, you must join us for Witchy Wednesday."

"I . . . maybe," I hedged. I didn't want to get in the middle of the witches' drama, but at the same time, I was interested. But in order to not commit to anything before I was ready, I turned the conversation back on her. "You won't be working here that night?"

She shook her head. "Oh, I don't really work here. My son owns the place. I just help him out when he's shorthanded."

"That's nice of you," I told her.

She looked down and sorted papers and bags around her till. I felt like she was hiding something. "I should really go and tidy up the produce section." She pulled her key from the cash register and turned to exit the till area. Now I was sure of it.

"How many nights per week do you usually help him out? Your son, I mean." I followed her across the store to the produce section, which looked fairly tidy. It was after eight at night, and the store was otherwise empty.

She spun on me, an apple in each hand. "Look, I'm here more than I'd like to be, but I'd appreciate it if you could keep that information to yourself."

The same way this town seemed to keep it to themselves that Lizzie was my aunt? I wondered if Marigold had gotten wind of that yet. I shrugged, because who would I tell, anyway? "Hey, I, of anybody, understand if you have to keep a job you don't particularly love in order to please your family. Where's your son tonight?" I looked around as though I might find him in one of the empty aisles.

She put the apples down and studied me for a long moment. She must have eventually seen something she thought she could trust because finally she said, "I asked my son if I could work during the week to make a little extra money. I'm here every night, but don't mention it around, all right? My fortunes business is not as good as it used to be, and when I'm here, I run into a lot of locals who need a little nudge to meet with me. If I'm out of sight, I'm out of mind, it seems."

As she explained this, I had a sudden thought. "Were you working Friday evening, then?"

She still looked sheepish as she rearranged the rest of the apples so their stems were all facing to the back. "Yes. Monday, Tuesday, Thursday, and Friday nights."

"And what time does this place close?" I glanced at the glass door, but it didn't appear to have hours listed.

"We close at ten."

Being here until ten, maybe ten thirty after she counted up the cash, would give her an alibi for Friday evening when Maple May was killed. I was about to suggest this when I realized there was a good chance the store was empty then as well, so who would be able to place her here, especially if she didn't like telling the locals how much she worked at her second job?

"Hey, I heard a couple of the witches mention that goddess statue again at the café the other day. Maybe I'll drop by on the weekend to see it." This might force me to pay out some of my slim savings for a reading from her, but I was curious about that part, too.

But her forehead contorted. "Who was asking? Who was it?"

Her eyes were so intent on me, and I couldn't bring myself to throw any of the other witches under the bus, especially not Rachael. "Um, I can't remember who it was. You know, so many new names and everything. But I love special décor and statues. Being in the real estate market has made me develop an eye for that sort of thing."

I thought I was doing a decent job of calming the tension and bringing the focus back to me, but Marigold's eyes darted around the shop as though there were other invisible shoppers around us.

"But if this weekend's not good . . ." I started to back toward the door.

Finally, she shook her head as if she was shaking off the stress. "Look, I would like to see you this weekend, Tabitha, but I'm afraid I don't have that statue anymore."

"No?" I acted like the thought had never occurred to me.

She lowered her voice. "Again, I'd appreciate if you didn't tell the others, but I sold it to a local art dealer. I was short on money for rent, so it had to be done."

I nodded, pulled out my phone, and asked for the name of the art dealer. "Just so I can see what it looks like."

Reluctantly, she gave me the name. "But you won't be able to purchase it. I specifically asked her not to sell it locally."

I nodded with understanding of her embarrassment. But I left with the feeling that even if Marigold Weathers was hiding parts of herself, she wasn't hiding a murder. I'd be willing to bet if the two detectives I met looked closer at her, they'd be able to unquestionably prove her alibi and find the statue in question.

When I returned to the boat, I was pleasantly surprised to find the hot plate worked perfectly, despite its age. Also, when I reached to the back of the cupboard, I found a plate with swirls of yellow and orange that I always told Aunt Lizzie looked just like the sun. I could have sworn I'd dropped this plate the last time I visited. I had cried something awful about it, but Aunt Lizzie had seemed completely unbothered. Maybe that was because she knew she could somehow replace it locally.

It was a small thing, but enough to make me feel a shred of hope. Maybe things could still turn around for me yet.

My bad mood passed surprisingly quickly. By morning, I came to the understanding that my dad had probably been right. I might have worked for Brendan for another five years without him giving me a decent listing of my own. Even the listings I'd gotten myself, he'd ended up teaming me up with someone more experienced who had taken all the credit in the end.

I'd find another job when I got back to Portland. In this town and especially after a good night's sleep, I found all of it hard to worry about.

Besides, I had plenty to focus on in Crystal Cove. It took full effort from Frank, Dave, and me to hook up my aunt's boat to Frank's winch and keep it angled correctly to navigate it onto the small boat launch area he had available.

After we had it secured, Frank promptly left on a hiking tour he was leading up into the mountains. Apparently, he was one of several tour guides in the area. He did land and sea tours for tourists and kept busy between that and running the marina.

I found out there was an older couple in their fifties who stayed in one of the other houseboats in the marina through the summer. Many of the other boats were docked here and used for weekend excursions, but Frank informed me that I was the most regular company he'd had in a while.

As Dave got busy sanding the hull of the Lady of Fortune, I headed into town to try and grab him a chocolate croissant. Unfortunately, by the time I got there, they were already gone.

Avrum pointed me to a row of baked goods at the top of his display unit. "You should really try the nutmeg brown sugar coffee cake."

It sounded delicious, and the brown sugar crumbled topping looked thick and decadent. "Sure, give me two slices. Any of your lavender lattes available yet?"

"'Fraid not. Not sure when I'll get a chance to grind more lavender, but I really think you should try the cardamom coffee. It's a local favorite."

"Are you local, then? Have you lived in Crystal Cove a while?"

Avrum shook his head. "I moved here a couple of years ago from Seattle, you know, for a quieter lifestyle." I could understand that. He went on. "Listen, I'm sorry if I seemed abrupt the other day."

"Another one of your headaches?" I guessed. When he nodded, I reminded him, "I know it doesn't sound like much, but mint on the temples really does help."

He nodded. "You're right. I should try it. Now if you don't want the cardamom, how about a cinnamon latte?"

I considered asking after the star anise brew that Frank loved so much but then decided to go with Avrum's second suggestion, even if I wasn't quite ready to try his first.

I agreed and then waited at a nearby table while he made up my order. A handful of customers were on the upper level, but none of the Witchy Wednesday group that I recognized.

Maybe it would be worth coming to their meeting the next night to see if

Marigold had even offered her alibi to the others, and maybe to see if Ruth showed up.

Then again, there was a good chance I'd find out more about the case on my date tonight.

As the day wore on, I decided I wasn't in any hurry to get back home. Instead of being a tiny fish in the huge pond of Portland, here I felt like maybe not a big fish but an important one. One who could actually make a difference just by existing in this little seaside town.

After returning with the amazing nutmeg brown sugar cake that I'd barely been able to resist the second piece of, I left Dave to his sanding and decided to take a walk along the beach. I was surprised when Sherlock tagged along and didn't leave my side, even as I made my way over barnacle-covered rocks.

We were a good jaunt along the empty shore away from the marina before I started talking out loud to my feline friend. "If Marigold has an alibi and the sale of her statue checks out, and Ruth isn't strong enough to have moved Maple May on her own, who do you think killed her?"

Sherlock had left a dozen detective novels open on the floor of the boat but hadn't led me to any more clues within them. Meanwhile, I had filled the updated information I had on Marigold into my spreadsheet, but it still left me in a murky confusion about who might have killed Maple May.

I looked at Sherlock, who was actively avoiding the water, keeping to the upper edge of the rocks and looking like he didn't enjoy walking on barnacles one bit, but he still didn't answer. When he stopped and sniffed at a rock, I went to see what had him so interested.

I moved the rock aside, and there was a small blue stone among the coarse sand underneath. "Huh. Is this what you were after?" I held it out, but he had already moved along. Another twenty feet and he pawed at another one but then immediately lost interest when I uncovered it and pulled it out.

"Wait," I said, standing up and looking at the blue rock. "Do you think there are more crystals down here somewhere?"

He sat on his haunches and licked his front paw like this conversation bored him, but I was suddenly interested.

Maybe there were blue crystals surrounding this whole town. Perhaps that was why I felt so much calmer here than at home. Maybe it was why so many mystic types came here in the first place. I had another pang of missing Aunt Lizzie and wishing she was here to tell me all about these things.

I looked down at the cat. Maybe if I wasn't so afraid of communicating with him, I'd actually learn something.

"Did you ever look for blue crystals out here with Lizzie?" I asked.

Yes. The answer was quick and felt sad.

"Did you ever find any?"

Maybe. Or maybe not.

"Could it have been another beach?" I asked.

I didn't hear anything, which I suspected meant that he didn't know. Still, I liked the cat's company more and more each day. I had forgotten how nice it was to have someone—even some feline—to talk to.

After walking as far as we could go without either climbing trees or getting our feet wet, we headed back toward the marina and the Lady of Fortune.

"Maybe I'll talk Detective Thom into lending me a blue crystal on our date tonight," I murmured as we got close.

That was when I remembered my next problem: I'd never planned to stay this long in Crystal Cove. I hadn't planned to do much besides scrubbing a boat, inside and out.

Which meant I didn't have a thing to wear.

Chapter Seventeen

WHEN I RETURNED AND boarded the Lady of Fortune in dry dock, I had to climb a rickety ladder to get onto the main deck. I waved to Dave, who had the loud sander working against the port side of the boat. On my way back, I'd mentally cataloged everything in my small suitcase, and the most formal items I'd brought were some khaki capris and a peach T-shirt.

I'd already packed most of my aunt's clothes, which were too big for me and not my style, but I headed up to her bedroom to look through the boxes anyway. But it didn't matter how many times I held up a floor-length organza dress or a sparkly purple cape, I couldn't see myself in any of it.

I sighed and moved around the bed toward the small closet where I'd been keeping my suitcase. I barely had the door open when my gaze darted up to a single dress hung on the rack above my suitcase.

I furrowed my brow. I'd completely cleaned this cupboard out before storing my suitcase in here, I was sure of it. I glanced outside, in the direction from where I heard the sander. But why on earth would Dave have put a dress in the closet?

I surveyed the cream-colored sheath dress that had an open neck and a fitted waistline. It most certainly would not have fit my Aunt Lizzie, but it appeared to be close to my size.

I took a deep breath and let it out slowly. No one else had a key to my aunt's boat, but even if they did, why would they stock it with a new dress when I was clearly packing up? Had

Detective Thom been by, suspecting I wouldn't have anything to wear?

I pursed my lips. That seemed a little presumptuous of a man I'd only just met. Sherlock had followed me up to the bedroom and now lifted onto his hind paws to investigate the open closet. He sniffed at the cream dress.

"Where do you think it came from?" I asked my cat. Maybe he had a better idea than I did.

But the only word I heard in my head was Magic, and this time I couldn't tell if it had come from his mind or my own.

So what if it was magic? I quickly undressed and slipped the dress over my head, just to see. I turned to Lizzie's mirror on the back of her door, and sure enough, it fit me perfectly. Not only that, but it probably looked better on me than most of my own clothes at home.

That was curious.

I left it on and headed down to the lower deck, still undecided if I'd wear it tonight. If Detective Thom had dropped it off and Dave had slipped it into the closet so it wouldn't wrinkle, I was torn between whether this would be the type of move my dad would make to be controlling or simply a kind and helpful gesture.

I picked up my phone from where I'd left it on the table, noticing I had a missed text.

Running late. Can you meet me at Norma's on the Beach at 7? It was from Detective Thom. His text made it sound less than a formal date.

I texted back: **Did you drop by the boat today?**

He replied almost immediately. **No, sorry. Had you expected me? I've been out of town since this morning.**

My brow furrowed. I'd almost had myself convinced that he had been the source of the dress. But if not him, who?

I texted back my agreement about meeting him at Norma's and then stuck my head out the front deck. "Hey, Dave?" I called when his sander paused. He moved into view, the sander still in his hand. "Did anyone drop by while I was out?"

He shrugged. "I can't hear much over this thing."

I nodded and stepped out onto the deck. "You don't by chance know anything about this dress?"

His eyebrows shot up, and I suddenly felt shy as this young boy scanned my body.

I quickly added, "I mean, you didn't see anyone deliver it?"

He shook his head. "Nope. But whoever did has good taste. Looks good."

My face burned. I quickly thanked him and slipped back into the cabin to hide my embarrassment.

I headed back upstairs and looked around Aunt Lizzie's small bedroom for any other surprise items that may have appeared. I didn't see anything. But I also didn't seem to want to take the dress off, magic or not.

The restaurant was little more than two blocks of winding roads from my aunt's boat, but I didn't want to walk home after dark, and I didn't think I should count on a ride from my date if he wasn't picking me up, so I took my car. When the place came into view, I started to relax a little. With plenty of outdoor seating, filled with casually chattering locals and fire torches lighting the place up, it didn't seem like the fancy place I'd imagined when I'd first seen my new dress.

At the hostess station right inside the front door, I was greeted by a pretty girl who couldn't have even been eighteen. "Do you have a reservation?"

"I, uh, think so. I'm meeting Detective Thom?"

The girl's smile instantly took on a strained look. "Of course. His regular table is right this way."

He had a regular table? She led me to the interior of the restaurant, which was candlelit and much fancier than the patio.

"He always eats here?" I motioned to the corner table she led me to, having the sudden thought that he must have had the dress delivered, even if he was out of town. I wondered if I should ask for an outdoor table instead. He clearly hadn't arrived yet.

The girl, whose name tag read LAILA, nodded and said, "Always." She pulled out the chair I was expected to take, but a sudden obstinacy came over me as I remembered how he'd barked at all the other officers and firemen on the side of the road. That, paired with the new dress, made me want to find the upper hand in this situation before he arrived.

"I'm sorry, but it's such a lovely evening. Would you see if there's any room for us on the patio?"

Laila's eyes widened, but only for a second. "Yes, of course. Let me check." She turned and swiftly walked away. After having a brief conversation with a suited man who appeared to be her boss, she returned. "I found something for you outside. If you'll just follow me right this way." Her voice sounded robotic, and I hoped I wasn't going to get her in trouble for the change of plans.

After only five minutes at the outdoor table, a shiver hit me from the seaside breeze that was getting cooler by the minute. The dress hadn't come with a wrap or sweater of any kind, and my own coat hadn't matched well, so I'd left it on the boat. In Portland, all outdoor restaurants came with enormous propane heaters on their patios. Not Norma's. And the locals seemed to know that, as in the last five minutes several of the nearby tables had cleared and no new customers had been seated at them.

I nibbled my lip, thinking I'd probably been hasty in changing seats. Just as I scanned the patio, looking for Laila, though, I set eyes on Detective Thom instead.

He stopped to interrupt a nearby waitress as she spoke to another table. The waitress had that same strained smile toward him but nodded a second later and headed back into the restaurant. Then the detective strode toward me.

"I'm sorry I switched tables. It just seemed like such a lovely evening," I said in a nervous voice at the same time he said, "I'm sorry I was late. I'm afraid it couldn't be avoided."

Even though he'd put the waitstaff on edge since his arrival, his words sounded genuine. "It's fine," I told him. "I just got here."

"I'm glad." Before he could say anything else, the waitress arrived and passed him a small menu.

"The wine list you asked for, Detective." The girl looked older than the hostess, but not by much. The uniform at Norma's seemed to be black pants with white button-down blouses and high ponytails. This girl's name tag read RUTH, which seemed like an uncommon name to have more than one of in such a small town.

"Yes, thanks." He took the small menu and passed it to me. "Please, order anything you like. I'm not much of a drinker, but where the food is concerned, I can help you with what's best here."

The waitress stood nearby, as if she'd be willing to wait all night until I opened the menu and chose a drink. But I handed it back her way. "I'm not much of a drinker either. I'd just love a sparkling water, if you have some." In truth, I loved a glass of wine with dinner. It had been a staple in my family's home for as long as I could remember. But I wasn't about to blur my judgment in case the topic of blue crystals came up.

The waitress nodded, smiled a genuine smile at me, and was about to turn and leave, but the detective stopped her. "We'll take the surf and turf appetizer to share, please, Ruth."

"Of course." She hurried off.

I wasn't the biggest fan of a man ordering my appetizer without consulting me first, but I had to admit, this was yet another normalcy in my family home—with a dad who liked to control everybody and everything. And I did love a good surf and turf.

It also gave me pause all over again about the delivery of my new dress. "You don't know anything about this dress, do you?"

"I—" He looked confused, as if the question was throwing him. "It's lovely.

I'm sorry. I should have said . . ."

I waved a hand, feeling stupid. "No, no. I just found it on my aunt's boat today. It's not her size, and so I wasn't sure where it came from." With Detective Jameson, I may have made a possibly true joke about it appearing as if by magic, but it felt as though that wouldn't even get a chuckle from Detective Thom.

"Maybe it was a gift she had stored away for you?" he suggested. "It really does look stunning on you."

I blushed and thought that over. Maybe it had been there all along and I'd simply overlooked it. "Thank you." I had to change the subject, as any further questions about this dress would really start to feel like fishing for compliments. "So to what do I owe this pleasure, Detective?" I spread my cloth napkin on my lap, mostly to give me something to do.

"I thought it might be nice to get to know you, away from business endeavors." His smile twitched at the side. "And please, call me Aaron."

"So this isn't about the case?" I'd convinced myself that it was, so I hadn't even considered what we might talk about otherwise.

"Not especially, no." The twitch of his lip again, which now that I saw it for a second time, made me wonder if it was from nerves. "Although, we are making some headway on that front, thanks to you."

"To me?"

He sighed. "I'm afraid I can't say too much, but you leading us to the local witch group has been very helpful."

"Some of them are serious suspects?" I guessed.

He leaned in. "Several of them all want to blame one particular woman from their group."

"Marigold Weathers?" I whispered, wondering if he could tell me if I was on the right track if I guessed correctly.

He nodded. "But she has a strong alibi."

So someone must have been able to place her at the grocery mart that evening.

"There's another in the group with a shady past who appears to be the most likely suspect at the moment." He sat back in his seat, with the oversharing apparently over. "I'm just glad that you weren't somehow involved. And I'm glad you're still in town."

"But you had to go out of town today. Was that regarding the case?"

He nodded. "I had to drive up to Portland to question Maple May's family a little more thoroughly about her past and any contentions she may have had."

"But I thought her sister was here in Crystal Cove?" I thought again about a possibly jealous sister who had lived in the shadow of her beauty queen sister.

"Mmm, she is. I've had several discussions with her since Friday. She's a lot easier to get answers out of than her parents."

"Could there have been jealous feelings there?" I asked, a little surprised at how open he was being about the case after how brash he'd been when we first met.

Aaron shook his head. "I didn't get that impression. From what I hear, a lot of people back in Portland were jealous of Maple May, but her sister Sonya led a simple life running a knitting shop and would not have traded places with her for any amount of money."

"No?" I thought again about the hand-knit poncho Maple May had been wearing.

The waitress delivered my sparkling water and what looked like a cola for Aaron.

He took one look inside the glass and said, "I'd love some ice for this." His tone was curt. There was one lonely ice cube floating in the soda.

Ruth murmured, "Of course," and hurried off.

The interruption seemed to remind Aaron he probably shouldn't be sharing so much confidential information with me. He turned the questioning onto my aunt's boat and how the work was coming.

I'd barely started to answer when Ruth returned with ice. However, she did not bring menus, and soon, yet again, Aaron was ordering a meal for both of us. "You like salmon?" he asked.

I was glad he at least consulted me before our waitress had walked away. "I do . . ." I hedged because I wouldn't have minded seeing a menu to at least look at the options.

But Aaron simply said, "Their salmon is hands down the best in town, and I wouldn't want you to leave Crystal Cove without at least trying it."

I supposed I couldn't argue with that.

Once Ruth left, I tried to think of a way to bring the conversation back around to the case, but Aaron did it for me.

"You know, the most difficult part of this case is dealing with all the mystical clues." He waggled all the fingers on both hands when he said this. "I have to admit, I have a lot of trouble believing in that sort of thing, no matter how much we come across it in local crime."

"You come across it a lot?" I smiled something close to a genuine smile for the first time tonight. Maybe my communicative cat and dress appearances had nothing to do with me and were simply a strange occurrence from being in this town. "I've had a hard time with stuff like that in the past, too." I couldn't bring myself to tell him that my beliefs were changing, or at least softening, as of late. But I felt a lot of kinship with the detective in this moment.

"There are tactile clues, too. Like the tire screeches are too far from the body to indicate a hit-and-run, and the medical examiner found rope abrasions on her wrists as though the victim had been bound." He shook his head. "Jameson keeps coming back with talk about spells and those blue crystals though . . ."

"What have you figured out about the blue crystals?" I leaned in.

"Well, you may have been right about a hair comb. We found one not too far from Maple May's body, and I hadn't thought much of it, but upon further inspection, our forensics team thinks the blue crystals could have fit into the design of it." He squinted his eyes a little.

"I'm still not sure how you would have known the blue crystals might have fit with the comb. You're sure you didn't touch anything like that before we arrived?" His voice sounded more trusting than it had the night I'd met him, but now I wondered if this "date" was only a ploy to get me talking.

I shook my head. Growing up with a politician had given me plenty of observance of twisting the truth, but I didn't love telling out-and-out lies to a police detective. But what could I say? "Maybe I'd seen a comb like it with blue crystals in one of the local metaphysical gift shops," I suggested. "I was so shaken up when I first arrived, I can't be sure."

In truth, I'd only been in one metaphysical gift show since arriving in Crystal Cove, and that one doubled as a café.

Thankfully, Aaron bought that reasoning. "Maybe I'll bring some photos by tomorrow and see if that jogs your memory."

"It sure seems like those crystals are valuable. I'd love to have a closer look at one again."

Unfortunately, Aaron didn't take the bait on my suggestion and instead changed the subject. "Tell me, Tabitha, what do you do for a living up in Portland?"

"I'm a realtor," I said. At least this much was true. Rather than admitting I'd just been fired, I told him, "My aunt's boat is going to take longer to fix up than I anticipated, so I'm taking a leave of absence until I can get it done."

He smiled. "I'm glad—not that your aunt's boat is giving you such a headache, but that you'll be staying in town a little longer." His mouth twitched again.

The salmon turned out to be delicious, and while I couldn't seem to bring the conversation back around to the case and who else he suspected in it, I left with a pretty good idea that Ruth-without-the-last-name was the witch with the shady past.

Ruth-the-waitress, on the other hand, had a profitable night. While I'd thought Aaron had been a little on the rude and demanding side, he ended up leaving her a fifty-dollar tip on the table when we left.

When my surprise showed, he said, "Ruth's putting herself through college, and when someone works hard, I like to make sure and reward it."

Aaron Thom had a tough side, probably developed over time and with the harsh sides of humanity he came up against almost every day. But he definitely wasn't the worst guy in the world.

Chapter Eighteen

AFTER LEAVING THE RESTAURANT, I drove toward the marina but felt too restless to go back to the boat just yet. Talking about the case, and then having Aaron purposefully steer the subject away from the details, left me curious and angsty and with extra energy.

I drove up to Main Street and was surprised to see the grocery mart wasn't the only place open and busy after nine o'clock. Even through the front glass door, I could see The Heirloom Café was bustling with customers. It was too late for coffee, and I was stuffed full of salmon, but I couldn't help myself and pulled over.

I'd just duck my head in for a second and see if any of the local witch group happened to be around. I was barely through the door when a man's voice over a microphone echoed throughout the place.

"Ring, ring. Ring ring," he said. The man was probably in his fifties and had graying hair that hung past his shoulders. He was reading from a paper held out in front of him. "The bell rings, but not for me alone."

Some people were rapt on him. Others were conversing in quiet conversations. The last poetry slam I'd been to had been in college, and I'd only gone because a friend had assured me I'd enjoy it. I'd felt too out of my element to even hear a word that was spoken that night. Tonight was different, though. It had to be the town because even though reading or understanding poetry was about as far from my wheelhouse as understanding magic, I didn't feel bothered by it here.

In fact, I glanced around to see if I might find an empty seat.

Before I found one, Rachael and her striped tights bounded toward me. I wondered how well I'd have to know her before I could ask about her staple wardrobe item without her being offended.

"Tabby? I didn't think you came in at night," she said.

"I don't normally." I scanned the lineup of customers and then the rest of the seated patrons once more. Again, Marigold, Donna, and Ruth were all here, but the poetry microphone was set up where they usually sat, so tonight they were off to the side, still seated on the upper level. There were others with them, too. The two tables they sat around contained mugs and snacks and gift boxes, but I couldn't see what was in them from my distance. They were leaning in and whispering to one another, ignoring the poetry.

"I, uh, just thought I might stop in for a chamomile tea," I told Rachael distractedly.

"I have chamomile at my apartment." She motioned her head toward the door.

I looked one more time between the witches at the rear of the café and Rachael. I was tempted to stay, if nothing else to make myself feel as though I'd tried something new, even if I had no intention of going near the microphone. But one more look at Rachael told me she really wanted to talk to me. Maybe she had figured out something new about the investigation involving Maple May's death. If Ruth was here, she clearly wasn't under enough suspicion that the police had arrested her.

I figured I probably had more chance of getting a little information out of Rachael than I did out of the others, so finally I said, "Sure, okay. Let's go."

Out at my car, she walked toward the passenger side.

"Oh, you don't have your own vehicle?" I asked her.

She bit her lip and shook her head. "I keep taking my driver's test and failing. I don't get a lot of chance to practice."

"Oh. Okay." I clicked my unlock button to let her in. She wasn't quite my age, but she also wasn't sixteen. "Do your parents live here in town?" Maybe she was taking me to the family home to have chamomile tea. If I'd known that, I might have declined.

She shook her head from the passenger seat. "Uh-uh. I moved here three years ago to try to get my magic gifts straight. To be honest, I'm kind of the disgrace of my family at this point."

If only I could tell her I understood that more than she knew. My older brother was a lawyer and had recently joined the legal team of Jefferson, Lerner, and Chase. Their firm took care of my dad's office and any legal issues that came his way. My younger sister was in her second year of medical school.

I followed Rachael's directions a surprisingly long way from the café. "How did you plan to get home?" I was pretty sure Crystal Cove was too small to have a bus system.

She shrugged. "I can usually find someone to drive me. I just didn't want to stay around tonight. The witches were all talking about Detective Jameson and what he asked each of them. I had a feeling if I stuck around, they might figure out that I'd tipped him off." She darted her gaze toward me. "You won't say anything, right?"

"I don't even know them," I said quickly. It wasn't as though I knew her much better, but I kept that part to myself.

Finally, she pointed to a fourplex in a small cul-de-sac of a neighborhood. It was well-lit, and with three streetlights around the small street, it felt like the homey type of neighborhood I would expect from a town as small as Crystal Cove. She directed me to the second parking stall out front.

"You live alone then?" I guessed.

"Yeah. I got a good deal on rent in exchange for cleaning. I moved to Crystal Cove when I was sixteen. I finished high school online, and back then I worked at the Heirloom during the evenings to pay my expenses, but with this place, the cleaning is enough."

Up until this moment, I would have said Rachael needed parents to take care of her a lot more than I did—and yet, at twenty-seven, I still spoke to mine pretty much every single day. Meanwhile, she seemed to have been doing just fine all on her own since she was in high school. I found it ironic that she seemed to live so independently here in Crystal Cove, while I—a college graduate and an adult—couldn't seem to get out from under my father's thumb.

"So you just clean the rest of the fourplex now for work?" I followed her down a pathway and up a set of stairs to a second-floor apartment in the fourplex.

"The fourplex and a few other places. I thought cleaning would give me a good opportunity to practice my magic." She unlocked her door and let me into a tiny one-room studio apartment with her bed straight ahead, a tiny kitchen to the right, and a small velvet loveseat to our left. "Most of my cleaning jobs are within walking distance." She sighed and sounded discouraged.

"But no magic practice?" I guessed.

She headed for her kitchen and filled a kettle. "Every time I tried, it actually ended up making more of a mess, so I had to work extra hard to get them cleaned in time. One time, I tried a spell that actually collapsed the family's whole pantry. Canned goods and pasta everywhere! I tried to put back as many of the shelves as I could, and I told them I had no idea what happened and that it crashed down all on its own, but they still let me go the next day. Lately, I've been good and just practicing my magic when I have another witch around to help me."

Even though I had no idea what it would be like to be a witch with problematic powers, I did have a good idea of what it was like to be a young woman who seemed much less capable than what was expected of her.

"So the local witches are willing to help you?"

She did something between a head shake and a shrug and then reached in the cupboard for some tea. "Maple May always tried. She really wanted me to get a handle on my powers so we could open a booth together at the summer fair."

"The others not so much?"

She offered another shrug in response. I moved into her apartment, ready to take a seat on her loveseat, but then caught sight of the interesting artwork on the walls. It wasn't picturesque artwork, but more like decorative words. The word "Bloom" in the center of a canvas had blossoms erupting from it on every side. The words "Magic wand" were sleek and pointed on one end. Words were everywhere, on every single wall, low and high.

"Did you do those?" I asked, pointing to the "Bloom."

She nodded. "It's just a silly hobby. When I'm home alone at night, working on words makes me feel less lonely and less like trying to make my magic work on my own."

"No, they're beautiful, Rachael! You should sell them. Have you ever tried putting them up on Etsy or in one of the local shops?"

"You think so?" She looked at me all squinty-eyed, like she thought I was crazy for suggesting it.

"I think you should at least try. I'd buy one."

The whistle of the kettle interrupted me before I could ask more. By the time she poured our tea and brought them over to the living/bedroom, I decided if I'd been invited in, I should really ask some of my pertinent questions.

"Thanks." I sat on the loveseat, while she puffed a pillow against the wall and sat back on her bed, her striped legs folded in front of her. "So you said you talked to Detective Jameson, right? How did that go?"

Her face brightened. "Really well! You were right, he wanted to see my video, and he even got me to forward it to him. It sounded like he was going to bring

Ruth in for questioning, but he hasn't done that yet."

"No? How do you know?"

"Well, he questioned Marigold and Donna. When they looked at me, I told them he'd come by my place to question me, too, just so they didn't catch on that I had sent him their way."

"And what did Ruth say?"

"She told us how strange she thought it was that he hadn't contacted her at all. Marigold said that it was probably because she doesn't have her last name listed in the town directory and they hadn't located her yet."

"But the other witches kept talking about Detective Jameson after that?"

She took a sip of her tea and nodded. "They kept rehashing the same details over and over. At first I just told them he asked me the exact same things he asked them, but then one time I messed up, saying he'd shown up at my job, just like he'd shown up at theirs, and they wanted to know which house. I had to backtrack and say it had actually been at home. I think they believed me, but I figured I'd better get out of there before I said something else wrong, so I told them I have an early cleaning job tomorrow."

"So the witches all have other jobs besides their . . . witchiness?" I didn't know how else to put it, and I was curious if Rachael knew about Marigold working at the grocery mart.

"Pretty much. Most of them take shifts at souvenir shops on Main Street, I think, but they don't talk about it much."

"Even Marigold?" I asked.

Rachael leaned toward me a little and lowered her voice. "She works at her son's grocery store, but she wants us all to think she just does it to help him out once in a while when she can fit it into her hectic fortune-telling schedule."

"She doesn't?" I was surprised Rachael knew her secret. But then I thought again about how fast word had spread around town about my relationship to my aunt, and I figured I shouldn't be too surprised.

"She hardly has any customers anymore, so she needs the money." A smirk played at the edges of Rachael's mouth, like she was happy about this. Before I could ask more, she brought the topic back around to the case. "It was hard to tell if Detective Jameson thought Ruth was a serious suspect when I talked to him and showed him my video. Hopefully, he'll question her tomorrow."

I took my first sip of tea. She'd put a bit too much sugar in it for my taste, but I tried to hide my wince, as I didn't want to get off topic. "Do you think Ruth was jealous of Maple May? Or do you think she could have wanted to kill her because of that one threat?"

"Well, everyone was jealous of Maple May. I mean, not just the magic, but she was really pretty and really smart." That lined up with everything I'd learned about her so far.

"What did she do for work?" I asked.

Rachael leaned forward, away from the wall, and her eyes dropped to where she now let her feet hang from the bed. "She just gave tarot card readings. But she was really busy, so she didn't need another job."

That seemed like a pretty good reason for any of the other witches in town to be jealous. "Why do you think she was so much busier than the other witches?" I asked. "You said she had an arrangement with a local tour guide?"

Rachael peeked up at me through her eyelashes. "I think so. But I wouldn't mention that to the other witches if I were you."

"But Maple May never told you that this was the case?"

Rachael shrugged one shoulder. "She told me she was seeing one of the local guides and that it was a little tit-for-tat thing. But I never pressed her about what that meant because the others were already so crabby about it."

"Do you think she actually liked this tour guide? Do you think he might know who wanted to kill her?" I still had suspicions that Maple May was killed by someone other than the witches I'd met my first night.

She shrugged her shoulder again and put her tea down. "She probably didn't have to date him if she didn't want to. She got perks wherever she went—extra toppings on her pizza or whipped creams on her drinks. She always got in free at the movies, and she even used to get gifts from a secret admirer."

Secret admirer? Now that seemed interesting.

But before I could ask, Rachael said, "Do you mind if we don't talk about Maple May anymore?" Then she yawned. "And, actually, I do have to get up pretty early."

I took the hint and got up to leave but asked Rachael if she would stop by and see me tomorrow at the marina after she was done with work.

As I drove home, I felt more of a sense of belonging than I'd felt in a long time—if ever. In Portland, I always felt like a nameless face, lost in the crowd.

In Crystal Cove, I felt like I could be important. Or at the very least, I could be a good friend.

Chapter Nineteen

I WOKE UP SEVERAL times through the night. My aunt's boat had been dry-docked on an angle, so it left me feeling uncomfortable in what was otherwise a gloriously comfortable bed. Plus, I guess I'd gotten used to being rocked to sleep each night. I didn't generally sleep well back in Portland, but I'd quickly become addicted to the idea of having a good night's sleep. I groaned in frustration.

I must have finally gotten back to sleep because the sound of Dave's sander woke me in the middle of another dream. This one included the group of all the witches I'd met, even

Maple May, all dancing in a circle. Maple May wore a comb with three blue crystals lining the top of it. Ruth had her face covered with a chiffon purple scarf. Marigold and Donna passed a statue back and forth that looked like the ones I'd seen when googling Destiny Goddess Statues. They were dancing on wisps of snow. And in the center of the circle . . . a single chocolate croissant.

I sighed as I pushed myself up to a seated position. It was becoming clear exactly what these dreams were: they were me trying to process all the information I had figured out so far about Maple May's death.

This was also a good reminder to open my spreadsheet and write down all the new information I'd come up with the day before.

I wasn't kidding myself. I didn't think I'd be able to solve this investigation when the local police force couldn't. But an inkling deep inside me still held to the hope that I might be able to help.

I checked my phone, and it was already after ten.

"So much for the chocolate croissants," I murmured to Sherlock, who had taken to sleeping beside me on my aunt's bed ever since we'd become more communicative with each other.

Sherlock stretched and wriggled his nose, like he didn't understand the appeal.

Of course he wouldn't.

I set up my laptop on the table and, while it booted up, thought of all the new entries I would add. Sonya Doerksen would get added to my list of suspects, even if Aaron didn't see her as one. Ruth would move to the top of the list, as it sounded as though she didn't have an alibi for the night of Maple May's death.

Then again, she didn't seem strong enough to have moved Maple May on her own. I wondered if she had a husband or a boyfriend. I typed that in with a question mark.

After logging in all of this, I sat back with a huff. For all I knew, Ruth didn't even have a last name. How was I supposed to be a help if I didn't even really know these people?

Beside Marigold's name, I marked the words "alibi" and "statue" along with the grocery store name and the art dealer who supposedly had her statue.

Under suspicious items, I now had: blue crystals, hair comb, Destiny Goddess Statue, and a car that had screeched to a stop at a distance from the body.

I had no idea how to check tires to see if they'd screeched to a stop recently, but the only person this piece of evidence ruled out was Rachael, as she didn't drive.

My stomach gurgled, so that was my cue to close my computer.

When I'd come back to the boat last night, it had been dark and it had been all I could do to get myself up the stepladder and into my odd-angled bed. But this morning, as soon as I opened the cabin door, I could see how much Dave had accomplished the day before.

"Is this whole side done?" I asked. There were patches of some kind of primer to cover up the spots that had been heavily rusted. It looked like an eyesore now, but I'd once been a student painter for a summer and could recognize the motley beginnings of what would be a beautiful finish.

Dave put the sander down and wiped his brow. "'Sposed to start raining tomorrow, so I thought I'd get as much done before then as I could. I set up a light and kept working until late."

"Wow, thank you!" I told him. "But don't you have school?" I had been so consumed with my thoughts of getting the boat finished, I had ignored his possible conflicts.

He nodded and grabbed his water bottle for a swig. "When I told my shop teachers about my project, they wrote me a note to get this week off. I'll work until it's done."

His declaration made me feel bittersweet. Now that I didn't have a job to get home to, I wasn't in such a rush to get the boat up for sale. I hoped it would at least earn Dave some extra credit. "So your shop teachers like that you're working on this?"

"Oh, yeah. I'm showing them pictures at each stage. Hey, would you mind taking a couple? Don't want to get dust all over my phone." He motioned to where his phone was tucked into a Ziploc along the boat launch.

I headed down the stepladder and grabbed for his phone, about to ask for the passcode, but then I saw he didn't keep it locked.

Wow. Small towns.

I took several photos, close-ups and ones that captured the whole boat. But when I got around to the other side, it looked as though he'd barely started. Then I had an idea.

"Hey, I'm happy to help paint, if you want to keep sanding. I once had a job painting houses."

He shrugged. "Sure. Rest of the paint's by the office." He motioned toward the dock entrance.

"Okay, great. I'll just have to change first. What do I owe you for the paint and the primer?"

He shrugged. "You gotta go pay Happy Hardware. I told them you'd come in and pay for it later."

Again, small towns.

Half an hour later, I was in the oldest clothes I'd brought—which weren't all that old—and had all the painting supplies down at the boat launch and was ready to start. I had to admit, I was a little disappointed not to see any special painting clothes hanging in my aunt's closet.

"I got the enamel-based paint, 'cuz it's the cheapest and you said you just wanted it nice enough to sell," Dave told me as I looked for the dry time on the cans.

"Okay, thanks." Again, that pang of bittersweet hit me as I thought of getting closer to selling the Lady of Fortune. "Looks like we can only get one coat in before the rain." This, at least, eased the pressure.

"You're going to want to start at the top and work your way down." He sounded a little less pleasant. I wondered if he was concerned that me helping would interfere with his teacher's grading.

But I was all ready to work now. I'd even forgotten about my grumbling tummy, and besides, it gave me a sense of satisfaction to think that I was going to be a part of making this boat better. But, if I was being honest, I kind of wished he'd sprung for the more expensive paint.

I got to work, and it was probably an hour later when Dave came back around my side of the boat to see how I was doing.

"Wow, you're a pretty good cutter." His pleasant mood was back. Maybe he'd just been concerned that I'd make a mess of it and he'd have to fix up all my mistakes.

"Like I said, I've done this before." I smiled at him.

He ran a hand over the one part I'd neglected to paint so far. It was the barely visible words labeling it the Lady of Fortune, with a few of the letters worn completely off. I didn't know why I couldn't bring myself to paint over it, but it was as if this was the last little part of the boat labeling it as my aunt's and I didn't want to cover it up.

Still, I needed to.

As if Dave knew this was my hesitation, he held out a hand for the roller. "Here, let me get that."

I passed it over—how could I not?—but as I did, a new thought excited me.

Before I had a chance to really mull it over, Detective Jameson interrupted us. I'd been so busy with my thoughts, I hadn't noticed his approach.

"I just had a few more questions for you." He looked from the stepladder to the door to the cabin. "Are we able to talk inside?"

I shrugged. "If you want to." It wasn't soundproof, but if it gave him a sense of freedom to talk about the case, who was I to argue?

He wore jeans and a sweater again today, so I wondered if he was working undercover or on his day off. He made an extra effort not to get fresh paint on his clothes as he went up the ladder, but me? I was already too speckled to worry about it.

We were barely inside when I realized the real reason he'd wanted to board my aunt's boat. Only a second later, he had her crystal ball in his hands, stroking it. Unlike last time, when I'd been so unsure about everything in this town, now I knew it bothered me.

"Can you please put that down, Detective?"

He raised his eyebrows at me but did as he was told. "Call me Jay. I heard you went out with Detective Thom last night." He nibbled his lip. "You two are seeing each other?"

Was he . . . jealous? No, couldn't be. "We just went out once," I told him honestly. "And we mostly talked about the case."

"Well, that's why I came by, too," he told me, straightening his sweater as though he momentarily forgot he wasn't in his suit. He seemed much more formal today than the last couple of times we'd talked. "I thought you'd like to know that Ruth Boudreau has a criminal record. I wanted to thank you in person for the tip."

Chapter Twenty

BOUDREAU? I had a last name. It was all I could do not to pull out my laptop and type it in right that second.

"So what did she do?" I asked instead. I could make notes later.

"I'm afraid I can't tell you that. In fact, I should really go." He took one more long look at the crystal ball. If I thought it would help him solve the case, I'd probably let him hold it some more. But that wasn't the case last time, and I was still on shaky ground about all the strange happenings I'd been experiencing on my aunt's boat.

I followed him outside and was pleased to see Dave had finished up the small bit of painting I hadn't completed, and I hadn't had to watch him do it.

"Are you free for dinner tonight?" Jay's voice was casual, and yet I felt some stress behind it. I supposed it made sense—if he thought I was already dating another detective, asking me out was a bit of a risk. But why me? Was he trying to pry more information out of me, or was an out-of-towner that much of a novelty to the local police?

I didn't want to get in the middle of two detectives, regardless. In fact, even though Aaron suggested he'd be in touch to go out again, I figured I'd be best to say no to both of them.

But today I at least had a nice way to decline Jay. "Actually, it's supposed to rain tomorrow, so Dave and I will probably be working until late to try and get as much accomplished on the outside of the boat as possible."

Dave was on the other side, sanding again, and so he wouldn't argue, even if sanding at this point was a one-person job.

Jay nodded. "Is it okay if I call you in a few days?"

"I—uh, sure. But I still don't know when I'll be heading back to Portland." Hopefully, the mention of me leaving would help him back off.

It did, at least for the moment, and he said goodbye.

As soon as he was out of view, my stomach let out a loud grumble. Thank goodness it held off, or he might have talked me into going for lunch right here and now.

I rounded the boat. "I'm going to head up to the café for a snack and a long-overdue coffee. Can I get you anything?"

When Dave saw me, he turned off the sander to hear better. "Yeah, that cake thing you brought the other day was pretty awesome."

The nutmeg brown sugar spice cake. Now my stomach growled twice as loud. "Sure thing," I told him.

I stopped at Happy Hardware and settled up my bill there first. It was a little more than I'd expected—apparently even the cheapest marine paints were pricier than house paints—but still far less than I'd originally thought it might be.

After that, I headed to the café. While I waited for Avrum to make up the cardamom coffee he'd finally talked me into and pack up a half dozen slices of nutmeg brown sugar cake, I looked around and was surprised to see Ruth sitting by herself.

I hesitated, then walked toward her. Maybe it was a matter of being surrounded by detective novels or waking up from strange dreams, but I couldn't seem to stop trying to find out the truth about Maple May's death. And if Jay wasn't going to tell me more about this witch's criminal record, maybe I could get it out of her myself.

As I got closer, I could see the worry lines that etched her face. She'd been tearing apart more than one paper napkin, and the pieces littered the wooden table in front of her.

I thought back to my dream. Had that been wisps of snow at their feet . . . or shreds of napkin? I shook it off. What did I think, I was some kind of prophet predicting the future?

"Ruth? Is that you?" I asked, even though I knew it was. Even though her appearance was quite forgettable—brown wavy hair that matched her brown coat and plain jeans—the fact that she was a witch who looked like this made her stand out in my mind. Plus, I had some idea now why she wanted to remain forgettable. Keeping her last name a secret because of a criminal record seemed like a pretty good reason.

She turned her downcast gaze up to me. "Oh. Hi. Tabitha, right?"

"Are you okay?"

She shook her head and shrugged at the same time. It was the first time I'd seen her look unsure of herself. "I—I don't know."

"Do you want to talk about it?" I reached for a chair and looked at her in question. She nodded so I sat across from her.

"It's just . . . I think I'm being investigated for Maple May's murder."

Even though I already knew this information, I pulled away from her like it was a surprise. "No. Not you?"

She nodded. "And the worst part is . . . I can't tell the police where I was that night, so I'm sure I look completely guilty to them!" She split the napkin she was holding in half and threw it down on the table between us.

"Why can't you tell them where you were? I mean, I'm sure it would help if they knew you couldn't have been out on the roadside when Maple May died." Unlike me, who was at the scene of the crime. Part of me still wondered if the two detectives were both trying to date me only to keep me under surveillance.

Ruth dug her fingers into her dark hair and pulled at the roots. "I already told them I was home alone that night, but they checked with my neighbors and they told the police my car was gone."

Her voice became more frantic with each word.

I felt guilty for pretending to be a confidant when I was truly just trying to find out more about the case, but at the same time, if she was a criminal and hiding something, it was for the greater good that I dug into it to find out what I could. I figured it might be easier to get to some parts of the truth if you weren't on the police force. The more I watched Ruth's stressed reactions, though, the more I thought she would have been much more obvious about her stress the morning after the murder when I'd first met her than she had been if she'd actually killed somebody.

"So were you gone somewhere with your car, then?" I dropped my voice quieter, trying to let her know she should trust me. She nodded but needed prodding to answer. "Where did you go that night?"

She studied me for a long moment before leaning in. "I went to go see my little boy in Salem."

I kept my voice equally low in hopes she'd keep talking. "Why don't you just tell the police that?"

She shook her head. "I can't!" she exclaimed in a stressed whisper. "There's a restraining order against me." I tried not to show my shock as she went on. "It was two years ago. I knocked into him, and he fell down his stairs and broke his collarbone. It was an accident, but Liam was angry with me at the time because I'd put him on a strict diet. He was having awful reactions to certain foods, but of course a four-year-old doesn't understand those sorts of things. He only thought I was depriving him, and he wanted to go back to his dad's house where he could eat anything he wanted."

She gritted her teeth together, momentarily more angry than worried. "My ex and I weren't getting along to begin with, and so he chose the moment at the hospital when the doctor had just explained little Liam's injuries to report me to the police. He coerced Liam to say that I'd pushed him, and so he finally got what he wanted—full custody, with a restraining order against me to boot."

I felt bad for her, but at the same time, I wondered if I could completely believe her story. I looked at her extra-large coffee cup, now empty. The caffeine probably wasn't doing her anxiety levels any good.

"What happened when you went to see your little boy?"

She shook her head. "I didn't even talk to him. I watched him through Johnny's living room window—that's my ex. Liam was so big, and I couldn't believe how much I'd already missed of him growing up."

"Still," I said softly. "Wouldn't it be better to get in trouble for disobeying a restraining order than to be charged for a woman's murder?"

"But what if they make the restraining order longer? I pled guilty just so Liam wouldn't have to go to court. I've been going to therapy, even though I never pushed him in the first place. I've been working so hard to be able to see him, but what if I can never see my Liam again?" Even though she kept her words quiet, she sounded frantic with worry.

"Did anyone see you outside your ex's place?" I asked. It might be useless information anyway if it didn't provide a good alibi.

She nodded. "The neighbor saw me, and she must have called Johnny because seconds later, he was at the window. He held up his phone like he was going to call the police and report me, but then I left right away, so I'm pretty sure he didn't."

An angry ex would make a pretty good alibi, and why wouldn't he admit seeing her outside? Unless he still held a grudge and he knew it would implicate her in a murder. "I really think you should tell Detective . . ." I hesitated but then decided on the gentler of the two detectives I'd gotten to know. "Jameson. Explain where you were and that you didn't try to get close to Liam. Have him question your ex without mentioning the Maple May investigation. I honestly think the police want to get to the truth behind a murder in Crystal Cove a lot more than they'd want to punish you for breaking the rules with your restraining order."

"Maybe," she said. And it seemed like she really was thinking about it. Regardless, I hadn't made any promises not to tell one of the detectives myself, so if she didn't come clean, I would. If it would help them solve a murder case and not keep them looking at the wrong people, it was worth breaking the trust of a woman I'd just met.

Because I didn't want her to suddenly think of this and make me promise to keep it to myself, I changed the subject. "So back to Maple May . . . if you weren't in town and couldn't be responsible for her death, who do you think killed her?"

Ruth took a deep breath, let it out slowly, and said, "I don't know. All the other witches keep whispering that it was Marigold. She was definitely jealous, but she says she has an airtight alibi for that night and she's already told the police."

"Okay, so if not Marigold, who? Do you definitely think it was another witch, or could it have been someone else in town or even a tourist?"

Ruth squinted. I got the impression she was relaxing a little now that the subject was diverted from her and her transgressions. "Well, I heard rumors that she was dating a local tour guide in exchange for promotion."

"Dating? Do you know who that tour guide was?"

She shrugged. "I don't know, but I know Frank from the marina took tourists to her tarot card shop all the time and I'd seen them having coffee together here more than once."

Frank from the marina?

This new suspect was a lot closer to home than I'd hoped.

Chapter Twenty-one

I OPENED MY MOUTH to ask Ruth more about the relationship between Frank and Maple May when Avrum called out, "Tabitha? Your order is ready."

My order had taken an unusually long time, but I suspected Avrum had noticed our deep conversation and had given us an extra minute. Now that Ruth had pulled herself together, he was willing to interrupt.

I held up a finger for him to wait, but Ruth said, "It's okay. Go. I have some things to think about."

So did I. Like how long I should wait before calling Jay or Aaron to let them know Ruth may have a strong alibi. Or what Frank had to say about his relationship with Maple May, who seemed a good twenty years younger than him. He'd been surprisingly detached when he spoke about the "dead witch I'd found on the road" the other day.

"Feel free to drop by the marina if you ever want to talk," I told Ruth before heading to meet Avrum at the counter. "Smells wonderful. Thank you," I told him.

"You bet. Working on the boat again today?" As he passed over the tray with my coffee, nutmeg cake, and a hot chocolate for Dave, I had a sudden idea. Back in Portland baristas were known for maybe not eavesdropping but just knowing things because they happened to be nearby making and/or serving coffee.

"I sure am. Dave and I will be getting as much as we can done, trying to beat the rain. Do you know Dave? He's the marina owner's nephew." I figured this being such a small town, he must.

"Frank Markowitz's nephew? Sure. He's in here all the time, but haven't seen any of the Markowitzes in a few days."

"Actually, I've been bringing them coffees and treats as Dave's been helping me restore my aunt's boat. Frank's away on another tour." Before Avrum could end the conversation and get back to baking, I quickly added, "Hey, I heard Frank used to promote Maple May's tarot card reading business on one of his tours. Had they ever been in here together? I heard something about them being, like, together together?" I still couldn't picture them as a couple, but I watched Avrum carefully, just in case I was wrong.

His gaze dropped to the counter in front of him and his eyebrows shot up, like there actually might be something to this rumor. Then he nodded. "You heard right," he said in little more than a whisper. A second later, he moved over to the bakery case and started rearranging some of the sandwich halves, avoiding my eyes.

Maybe it was because I was from out of town. Or perhaps he didn't want to paint the late Maple May in a bad light. But this suddenly gave me a sick feeling, thinking of Frank, who hadn't seemed at all shaken up by Maple May's passing.

I reached for another thought—any other possible explanation. "Did you hear about Maple May having a secret admirer in town? Someone sending her gifts?" I leaned in, even though it seemed like he was moving farther away from me behind the counter. "Baristas hear things, right?" I asked, trying to draw him in.

But it didn't work. "I only know about Markowitz. Maybe you should ask him if he'd sent her gifts. Seems likely to me." With that, he turned with one of his sandwich trays and moved toward the rear counter, clearly done with this conversation.

And I felt like an outsider in town all over again.

On my short walk back to the marina, I deliberated between questioning Dave about his uncle or calling Jay or Aaron about Ruth's alibi. Jay seemed like the safer bet. While I appreciated Aaron's attention to the tangible details, I had a feeling he was also a very by-the-books detective and may not be in favor of keeping Ruth breaking her restraining order quiet.

I had pretty much settled on calling Jay first and then striking up a conversation with Dave afterward, when I descended the slope toward the boat launch and saw Frank heading into his office.

He was back? As much as I dreaded doing it, the more responsible action would be to ask Frank a few pointed questions while I had him here. He was all decked out in what looked like a well-equipped fishing vest, so I had a feeling he wasn't going to be sticking around long.

When I got to his shack, I reached across the water to knock, but before I could, the door swung open, almost knocking me across the dock and into the other side of the water.

"Oh! Wow. Frank. You're here." I tried to catch my breath and come up with my words all at once, but I wasn't having much success.

"Not for long. What's up, Dave having problems with the boat finishing?"

"No, no. Dave's doing great!" My voice sounded overly peppy. I brought it down a notch. "Where are you off to?"

"Just got word about the storm moving in. I was going to start a hiking tour from the beach here, but instead, I'm going to meet my tour participants up at the cabin so we don't miss our window of decent weather."

He had a cabin as well as a marina? But that part wasn't important if he was in a hurry to get out of here. "Listen, Frank, I just had a quick question about Maple May Doerksen. The woman who died on my way into town the other night?"

He blinked a couple of times but didn't show any emotion. "What's up?"

I ran my hand along the edge of the coffee tray, wondering how to phrase this properly. But I didn't have time for a lot of careful wording. "Word around town was that the two of you were seeing each other?"

He pulled back. "Are you crazy? She was a nice girl but way too young for me."

That was what I'd thought, but Avrum and Ruth . . . they'd both given me a different impression. "But you did promote her tarot card readings on your tours?"

He shrugged but started to move up the dock toward the parking lot, reaching down to grab a duffel bag on his way. "Sure. She was the best reader in town. Lots of tourists like that sort of thing and want the whole psychic experience, you know? I'm taking another couple of young witches who are looking for that same thing out tonight."

"Yeah, but you never went out with Maple May in exchange? You never even got a coffee with her?" If Avrum and Ruth were exaggerating, I had to know.

"Listen, Tabitha." His voice was suddenly deep and angry. "I don't know what you're trying to imply, but you're not from around here, and before you start blabbing ridiculous suggestions all over town, you'd better get your stories straight. If you need to talk about this, we'll do it when I get back from the camping store to pack up."

With that, he marched up to his truck, slung his bag in the back, and was driving off seconds later, without another word.

Chapter Twenty-two

I HEADED DOWN TO my aunt's boat and circled around it, but Dave was nowhere in sight. He took breaks for food whenever he got hungry, but I had the sudden sickening worry that he'd overheard my conversation with his uncle and he'd decided to no longer help me.

"Dave?" I called out. "Dave, are you around?"

I was greeted with silence.

"It's not that I was trying to imply . . ." I murmured to myself as I looked down at the sander, which had been placed on the ground on the side of the boat he had been working on when I left.

Mreaow . . .

I looked up to see Sherlock on the upper deck of the Lady of Fortune.

"Did Dave overhear my conversation with his uncle?"

Sherlock tilted his head, like he had no idea who or what I was talking about. And why should he? He was a cat. Sometimes I thought that cat held all the secrets to the universe. Other times, he probably didn't know his own name.

Still, I felt desperate for some reassurance that I hadn't screwed up. "The guy who was out here sanding the boat? An hour ago?" My frustration was showing, but I didn't care. Not only had he left the sanding and painting unfinished, but he'd also given me a list of mechanical parts that needed greasing or replacing—things I knew nothing about. My racing worries were suddenly cut off with a calm thought.

He told me he wanted pizza.

"Dave? He talks to you?" I asked the cat. I'd just assumed I was the only person Sherlock had regular conversations with.

Sherlock lifted a front paw to lick it. *Most humans talk to me. You're the only one who took a while.*

I squinted up at him. "They do?"

Most of them use childlike voices, like somehow they think I'll understand them better.

Oh, that kind of talking. "So you didn't talk back to Dave? Or to anyone?"

He tilted his head, like he didn't understand. But at least I had some hope that Dave hadn't angrily left the job half done. The spice cake would wait, but I wasn't sure what to do with Dave's hot chocolate. I supposed I could find a pot to heat it up when he returned.

I sighed and took a seat on the dock to enjoy the rest of my cardamom coffee. I wouldn't say Avrum was wrong, as the coffee was flavorful, but I still preferred the lavender and star anise varieties.

I looked up at the side of the boat I'd painted and figured it probably only needed one more coat. If only the rain would hold off long enough so I could do it.

I was lost in thought about all that still needed to be done before I could put the boat up for sale, when a voice called out, "You wanted to see me?" from up near the parking lot.

I recognized the striped tights, even from a distance, and I was growing to appreciate Rachael's wardrobe more and more each time I saw her. At least it was one thing I could count on in this town.

I'd texted Rachael earlier when I'd had my idea and asked her to drop by when she had finished her cleaning jobs. "Come on down here. I wanted to ask you something," I called.

She took in the marina and the skies and then made her way down toward me. "You heard there's a rainstorm coming?"

I nodded. "We're trying to get as much of the sanding, priming, and painting done before it does. But there's no way we'll get it all finished. It has to have time to cure between coats."

She folded her arms over her chest, surveying the side that at least had one coat of paint on it. The words "Lady of Fortune" could still faintly be seen on the stern of the boat. I'd been trying to pick up the different boating terms as I heard Frank and Dave use them.

I beckoned her that way. "See the name?"

She nodded. "Lady of Fortune?"

"It had been the boat's name when it was my aunt's, and even though I'm selling it, I don't know, it wouldn't feel right not to have it on here." When she tilted her head, studying it closer but not replying, I went on. "I hoped you might work some of your lettering magic on it. I'd pay you for it, of course. What do you think?"

She brightened. "You're sure?"

I nodded. "Nothing too crazy." Although, truth be told, even if she painted the words as ornately as the Blossom piece in her apartment, I'd still love it. It just may not be what a prospective buyer would want. "But I'm hoping you could do it as soon as the rain passes and I get a second coat on."

She dipped her head and said, "Sure, yeah." I recognized it as her not believing in herself or her ability as much as she should.

"It'll be great," I told her. "I know it will."

When she looked up again, her eyes were serious. "You know, I've been thinking what you said about Maple May. And what if the tour guide she was dating in exchange for promo found out she didn't actually like him and got really angry about it?"

I looked toward the parking lot and thought again of Frank. "I heard the owner of the marina used to promote Maple May on his tours of the town," I said, gauging for a reaction.

"Frank?" She lifted an eyebrow. "Well, sure. He was swept up in Maple May's charm, and if he hadn't been so old, maybe he would have thought she actually liked him."

I twisted my lips, unconvinced that his age proved any kind of innocence here.

"But did the two of them actually ever go out? Like on a date?"

She scowled. "I think she met him for coffee, you know, to talk over the details of promotions."

Rachael clearly didn't think this line of questioning was going anywhere. "What about that secret admirer of hers?" I wasn't convinced that Frank and the secret admirer weren't one and the same person. "Did she ever let you know if she had any idea who it was?"

"Oh, she had an idea. Apparently, he was going to meet with her to get his cards read, but I guess she didn't get a chance to because she was killed that night."

"She was supposed to meet with him the very night of her death?" Or maybe she met with him and that was why she was killed that night. "Who did she think it was?" I held my breath, not wanting to believe it could be Frank.

But Rachael shook her head at my question. "She wouldn't tell me. She said if it was who she thought it was, she wanted to let him down gently before anyone else found out."

"So she didn't like him back?" Again, I thought of Frank.

Rachael shook her head. "But she'd been excited, too. I think part of her hoped it would be someone unexpected. Someone she really did like."

All of a sudden, the sander started up on the far side of the boat, making me jump. There were a lot of ways to get to the boat launch, and I'd been so intent on my conversation with Rachael, I hadn't heard Dave's approach.

I wondered if he'd overheard any of our conversation. I hoped he hadn't walked up when I'd been questioning her about his uncle.

I decided to change the subject—to get the focus off the idea of any kind of tour guide or secret admirer being implicated in Maple May's murder. "Do you still think Marigold or one of the other witches was jealous enough to kill Maple May?"

She shrugged and nibbled her lip. "Probably not, but Marigold can get pretty jealous."

I started to lead her away from the boat and up toward the parking lot. She didn't have a car, so she must have walked from town. "Okay, but if Marigold was so jealous, wouldn't she have wanted to kill Lizzie more than Maple May?"

"Oh, she did want to," Rachael told me, which made me pull back, stunned. "But she knew Lizzie was too smart, and with all her magical crystals, she could just cast a spell of protection over herself."

"Magical crystals? Did Lizzie have a lot of those? I haven't found any on her boat."

Rachael shrugged. "I'm pretty sure Maple May had some of them. Not sure who else, but I'll bet there's been a dozen witches on that boat since she died, searching for Lizzie's most powerful pieces."

That was why I hadn't been able to find any. This led me back to believing that maybe one of the local witches was responsible for Maple May's death. Of course the crystals could have only been in Maple May's hair comb if my dream meant anything, which I was unconvinced about. "There are really a dozen witches in this town?" I asked.

"Oh, more than that. Plus, the ones who just pass through."

That one sentence made me feel like I was no closer to solving this than I had been the first night I'd arrived. "Are you headed back to the café?"

She shook her head. "I was between cleaning jobs. I got one of my clients to drive me into town, but I should probably get back."

If she'd come into town just to see me and what I wanted, I couldn't help but offer her a ride back. She was quick to accept.

But the whole way to her place and back, I kept thinking of Aunt Lizzie's blue crystals.

If Maple May had stolen some for herself, and if they were found at the scene of her murder, could she have been trying to cast a protection spell for herself?

I knew I had to call Detective Jameson, but now I wasn't sure what to tell him.

Chapter Twenty-three

IT DIDN'T TAKE LONG to get to Rachael's and back to the marina, but in that short time, Dave had packed up and left. The sander had the cord wrapped up and was locked up in the boat cabin, and the paint supplies were all cleaned up.

Worse, there was a paper sign on the office door that read, "GONE ON TOUR. BACK FRIDAY."

Frank had already come back and left as well? The sick feeling returned to my stomach as it all started to make sense. Dave had overheard us talking about his Uncle Frank. And he'd informed him of our suspicions.

So had he actually gone away on some kind of tour or was he only trying to escape questioning?

When I got inside the boat cabin, Sherlock followed me and confirmed in my thoughts that the old human had returned in a rush, spoken to Dave, thrown a bag together, and rushed off.

I fumbled over the bureau until I found Jay's business card and quickly typed his number into my phone. The second he picked up, I spoke in a rush. "I've found out some stuff about Maple May's death. Can you stop by the boat?"

Ten minutes later, he climbed the stepladder and stepped into the cabin where I was pacing. For once, he ignored the crystal ball and focused on me. "What is it, Tabby? What did you find out?"

"Did you hear from Ruth?" I asked first. He shook his head, but those details no longer seemed as urgent. "I think you're looking in the wrong direction with those witches. I think it's someone else."

He gripped my wrist to stop me from pacing. "Who?"

I shook my head, still not wanting to believe it. "Rachael told me Maple May had had a tarot card reading planned for the night she died. It was with a secret admirer." Before Jay could react, I went on. "Apparently, Maple May also dated a local tour guide in town in exchange for promotion for her readings. I'm worried that these might be connected or even the same person, and when she told him she didn't feel the same way about him, what if he got really angry about it?"

Jay nodded, studying me for several long seconds. "So this is all just conjecture?"

"Well, yes, but don't you think it's possible?" Then I went on to tell him about Frank's strange reaction to me and how Dave and Frank had both packed up and left quickly while I drove Rachael home.

He nodded slowly. "It does sound suspicious."

I was glad he thought so.

But then he said, "I guess we'll just have to wait for Frank to get back from his tour to ask him some pointed questions."

I furrowed my brow, the sick feeling in my stomach making me want to double over. Why wasn't he taking this more seriously? "But, Jay. He's taking more witches out on tour tonight—out to some cabin. He seemed panicked. What if he doesn't come back? Or what if he hurts them?"

With this, at least Jay seemed willing to look into it.

Chapter Twenty-four

THE REST OF THE afternoon, I rode around with Jay to the small police station in town and then out to Frank's and Dave's homes, both of which were vacant. Frank lived alone, and when we questioned one of the neighbors, we discovered Dave's parents were away on a holiday. Apparently, Dave didn't spend a lot of time at home and almost never returned before dark.

"I can't find any records of a cabin owned by Frank Markowitz," Jay told me after leaving the police station for the second time. This time, I waited in the car, as the last time when he'd brought me inside, it had brought up a lot of side-eyes about why Detective Jameson was hauling a civilian and her cat around with him to ask questions.

Yes, I'd brought Sherlock.

"Why, again, are we bringing the cat along?" he asked.

He had asked me this twice already. So far, I'd held him off with a response of, "You believe in getting answers from areas you don't quite understand, right? Just trust me on this one."

I looked at him with raised eyebrows. "We can leave him at the boat if you want."

He let out a sigh and started his car. "No, no. We'll bring him. I'm just not sure how Avrum will feel about us bringing him into the café."

"We're going to the café? You need coffee?"

Jay backed out and got onto the main drag that led to The Heirloom Café. "No, but it's Witchy Wednesday?"

"Uh-huh?"

He shrugged. "If we can't find Dave or Frank, there has to be someone there who'll know where to find them."

"One of the witches? Why would you think that?" I wondered if I was missing something. Did he think one of the witches had a special ability to locate people? Or maybe Frank had promoted others of them at various times. Or perhaps Dave was known for mechanical work on the local witch vehicles.

But Jay said, "Everyone who's anyone in Crystal Cove goes to Witchy Wednesday." He glanced at me to see I clearly didn't understand. "When you live in a small town, events aren't really optional. Everyone supports."

"Even those who aren't witches?" I asked, but then I thought of the poetry slam, which had the café packed with patrons, even late at night.

This made him chuckle. "You'll see. Even those who don't believe in witches will be there."

He wasn't kidding. The first nonbeliever I set eyes on was Detective Aaron Thom, who was seated at a small table near the front of the restaurant with two other uniformed police officers. The witches were at their usual tables near the rear of the restaurant, but now there were at least twenty of them, several wearing pointy hats or dresses that dragged on the floor, and Rachael was not the only person in striped tights. The rear of the café was lit by flickering candles, and the rest of the place was full, too, with a lineup of at least ten people waiting for hot drinks or pastries.

Jay headed straight for the cops. "We're on the lookout for the Markowitz boys—Frank or Dave. Anyone have a 10-20 on them?"

The two uniformed officers shook their heads, but Aaron's gaze bounced between me and Jay. I'd left Sherlock in the car for the moment. I avoided Aaron's eyes, as he had texted me an hour ago, but I'd thought my best bet in this case was to talk with Jay about the details I was learning.

"What have they done?" one of the cops asked.

"Maybe nothing," Jay said. "But I want to question them in regard to the Doerksen case, and I have reason to believe one or both of them may have headed out of town to a cabin they may or may not own." He shook his head. "I couldn't find anything listed."

"You should talk to Sheena Parks. Last I heard, Dave Markowitz was dating her little sister." The cop motioned to the witch group.

Jay nodded, and Aaron stood up. "I'll come along."

"It's all good," Jay said, slapping a casual hand on Aaron's shoulder, but he shrugged it off almost violently.

"I said, I'm coming along. It's my case." He pushed past both me and Jay and strode purposefully to the rear of the café. I raised my eyebrows in surprise at his sudden abruptness. Then again, he had acted similarly when I'd first met him.

He interrupted three witches who were busy talking. "Miss Parks, can I please ask you a couple of questions?" Aaron's voice wasn't loud, but the seriousness in it caused all the witches around to stop talking.

"Uh, yeah. Sure." The slight woman who must have been Sheena Parks was one of the witches wearing a black witch hat. I wondered if she, like Rachael, was trying to dress the part to make up for a lack of magical prowess. She moved close to a wall, but it still wasn't very private, as there were people everywhere tonight.

Rachael intercepted me before I could follow them. "Tabby! You came for Witchy Wednesday!"

"Well, yes, but I may not be staying." I glanced to where the two detectives had cornered the witch.

Rachael didn't miss my split attention. "Is this about the case?" she whispered. "Does Sheena know something?"

I shook my head. "I don't know, Rachael, but I'll let you know when we figure out anything. For now, you should get back to your friends. Do you have a ride home?"

She nodded. "Avrum said he'd drive me when he closes up. I thought I could pepper him with some questions about Maple May's secret admirer on the way. You know sometimes coffee baristas overhear things."

I didn't want to tell her I'd already had the same idea and covered that. If this would make her feel useful in her friend's investigation, why not let her? Besides, if all went well, we'd be back with Frank in handcuffs before she even heard what Avrum had to say about him.

"Good idea," I told her. "But for now, I should go. Come by the boat tomorrow and I'll give you an update."

By the time I caught up to Aaron and Jay, Aaron had clearly asked a few questions.

"Well, yeah, sure, Dave's been over at our place with Judy a few times, but he won't be there tonight."

"No?" Aaron asked. "Why not?"

"When Judy first moved in with me, I set the rules that no boys were allowed in our apartment when I'm not home."

"Could Judy be out with him somewhere?" Aaron asked. His tone was all business, but at least he didn't seem as rude as when he spoke to his fellow officers.

Sheena shook her head. "She has a biology project due tomorrow. She couldn't even make it to Witchy Wednesday because she's got so much work left on it to do."

"And what's the address of your apartment, Miss Parks?"

She crossed her arms. "Is Judy in some kind of trouble? Or Dave? I told her I didn't trust those Markowitzes."

"No, no. Nothing like that." Aaron spoke as though he knew exactly what was going on, even though he hadn't even taken five minutes to find out the details of what Jay knew. "We just think he may have some information regarding a case. We'll just stop in on Judy and see if she happens to know where he's at tonight."

Sheena glanced around. "Oh. Okay. Well, should I go with you?"

"No need, Miss Parks. Thanks so much for your help." Aaron strode toward the front door of the café, and Jay and I followed.

"Can't we just call Judy and ask her where he is?" I asked as we reached the outdoors. It was chilly out, but at least the rain hadn't started yet.

"Oh, he's there," Aaron said, heading for his car. "Fifteen-year-olds doing biology homework is the oldest excuse in the book."

Chapter Twenty-five

I HATED TO ADMIT it, especially when he was acting so cocky, but Aaron was right. Jay and I had followed Aaron to the address in Jay's car, and only seconds after Aaron banged on the apartment door and called out, "Open up! This is the police!" a young teenage girl opened the door, straightening her T-shirt, with lipstick smeared across her face.

"Hi. Um, what can I help you with, officers?"

Jay and Aaron were both dressed in suits. I wouldn't have assumed they were police officers if they'd shown up at my door, but then in such a small town, everyone likely knew the local detectives.

"We're looking for David Markowitz." Aaron's deep voice, in conjunction with his ever-moving stance and roaming eyes, quickly made Judy come under his authority.

"He's inside. Um. He just stopped by to drop off—"

"Save the excuses." Aaron held up a hand. "We just need to speak to him for a moment."

The relief I felt that Dave Markowitz hadn't left town with his uncle was palpable. Judy disappeared into her apartment, and we waited out some panicked whispering from inside before he appeared.

"Hey, dudes." He said this casually, even though he hadn't seemed friendly with Aaron or Jay when they'd dropped by my aunt's boat—at least not friendly enough to say hello. I wondered if it was an act to prove some kind of innocence. "You need to talk to me? What's up?"

Aaron stepped back and held a hand out to Jay, suddenly out of his depth with information. I had Sherlock snuggled in my arms, and he started purring. I wasn't sure if he was trying to send me a subliminal message that Dave had so little to hide that it was calming my cat or if my warm arms were simply putting him to sleep.

Jay didn't hesitate to take over the interrogation. "We're actually looking for your Uncle Frank. Any idea where he might be?"

Dave shrugged and seemed to see me for the first time. "He left on a tour this afternoon. You saw him," he said to me.

"Yes, but he didn't say exactly where he was headed. A cabin somewhere," I started to say, but Aaron cut me off with a staccato word and one held-up finger.

"Ah." He turned to Dave. "And do you know where he'd be on this tour?"

Dave shrugged again. "I think sometimes he borrows a cabin from his hunting buddy up on Crystal Mountain. He's probably up there getting everything ready for the girls."

"The girls?" Aaron looked to Jay to see if he knew what this meant. Jay kept his gaze squarely on Dave while the sickening feeling in my stomach intensified.

"Sure. He's taking two tourists up the mountain on a Vision Quest at midnight. Usually they hike from here, but because of the weather, he said he'd meet them at the cabin. I think they're both witches."

Aaron's gaze narrowed. "And do you know where to find this cabin?"

"Nuh-uh. But there's prob'ly info in his office. Uncle Frank keeps good records."

"I'm sure he does," Aaron said, taking Dave by the arm. "Now why don't you tell us all about this 'Vision Quest' on our way down to his office."

Chapter Twenty-six

AS WE LEFT JUDY'S apartment building, Aaron announced, "I'll take Dave in my car. I'll meet you at the marina, Jameson." His eyes glazed over me, but I didn't take offense, as there were much more important things going on.

Jay nodded. "Sure thing." I thought I could hear a note of frustration behind his voice, but he didn't argue and led me toward his car.

I wasn't sure why Aaron thought he needed to help in the first place. Jay would have been perfectly capable of asking a couple of teenagers a few questions.

Regardless, seconds later, Jay drove us back toward the marina. We followed Aaron and Dave down the dock and to his uncle's office and then watched as he located a key along an upper eave and opened the door for us.

"Uncle Frank keeps all his records in that file cabinet," he said, pointing. Aaron marched directly for it before Dave had a chance to add, "But he was in a hurry, so I'll bet this one's still on his desk somewhere."

Aaron's eagerness left Jay closest to the desk in the corner of the small floating office, so he headed there. It was littered with papers, and even though Dave had already turned on a dim overhead light, Jay used a small flashlight to illuminate the desk.

I avoided Dave's gaze, even though I felt him staring at me. He had been such a help to me with the boat, and Frank had made it all happen in the first place. Then again, if Frank had killed Maple May—and worse, if others might be in danger from him—what choice did I have?

"I think I found it," Jay said.

Both Aaron and I moved closer. Dave stayed near the doorway, his eyes darting between all of us at regular intervals.

"Does it say where the cabin is?" I asked at the same time as Dave said, "What's the big rush? He'll be back Friday. Is Uncle Frank okay?"

"Oh, I'm pretty sure your uncle is just fine," Jay said and then angled a booking sheet so that Aaron could see it. I was between them, so I got a good look at it as well. "They were meeting at the cabin at nine. It has an address, so it must be drivable. And it appears these are his two tourists."

Jay held a finger near the two women's names. Amy Litke and Selma Mack. Beside each of the names, Frank had scrawled the word "Witch!"

Jay and Aaron looked at each other for a long moment, clearly thinking about what this might mean.

Then Jay pulled out another page from beneath that one. "The part that bothers me is this topographical map.

They're clearly heading to this destination for midnight tonight, but I have no idea how to track them in the dark."

"I can!" The words burst out of me. When I'd first decided to go into real estate, my first inspiration was to become an expert in unusual properties —the ones out of town and on mountains and halved by streams. I'd taken a very hands-on course in topography and had really enjoyed learning about it until my dad insisted that the real money was in urban properties and development. I pointed to the map. "Look, it's only a few miles' hike, and the terrain doesn't look too bad."

There could be a lot of foliage, but if Frank and these two women were going in ahead of us, I expected there to be somewhat of a clear path. I was just glad all my years of not knowing what I wanted to do with my life and exploring all my options could be useful for once.

Silence filled the small office. What were they waiting for?

"Should I come, too?" Dave asked, finally breaking the silence.

Aaron shook his head. "Stay here and keep your phone on in case we need anything else from the office."

Jay plugged Dave's cell phone number into his own phone, while Aaron added, "We shouldn't bring any civilians along."

Was that the issue?

"Look, honestly, I can do this. I've done this before." I wanted to be a help so badly that my desperation leaked out in my voice.

As Jay scooped up the papers for Frank's tour to bring them along, I saw another sheet labeled, "Packing List."

"Hang on." I pulled the packing list toward me. "Why would he need a steel-headed ice ax?" I looked at Jay and Aaron, but when neither of them had an answer, we all looked to Dave.

He shrugged. "Dunno. He probably always brings his climbing gear in case he can't get to where he's going."

It was a vague answer that didn't make much sense. What worried me more, though, was that I knew the shape of an ice ax. It was the term I'd been looking for when I'd been describing the shape of Maple May's body to the group of witches.

And if it had a steel handle, it could have doubled as a weapon to give her a contusion on the back of her head.

He'd brought the ax along on this tour with two witches for a reason, and I had a feeling it had nothing to do with getting to wherever he was going.

Chapter Twenty-seven

THE ROAD WAS PITCH-BLACK, lit only by Jay's headlights as we made our way up the mountain road toward the cabin. His sedan wasn't made for the potholes, mud, gravel, and tree branches we came across, and so we had to take it slow—less than ten miles an hour at some points.

Aaron seemed to have known this, suggesting we take Jay's car from the onset. As Jay drove, he filled Aaron in on everything we suspected and the intel we'd already gathered from Ruth, Rachael, and Avrum about Frank and

Maple May's history together. Aaron made notes on his phone.

From the back seat, I checked the time on my phone. It was already ten o'clock. I ran a hand over Sherlock's fur, and he purred in response. I hadn't brought the cat on purpose on this leg of our journey. He'd just hopped into the car after us at the marina, and I hadn't stopped him. I figured once we reached the cabin, if Frank and his tourists had already left, Sherlock could wait in the car.

"You said Ruth Boudreau has a strong alibi. Tell me more about that?" Aaron said.

Jay motioned over the seat to me. In the darkness up here and with Jay looking at the road in front of us and Aaron studying his notes, I didn't feel quite as bad for sharing Ruth's secret. But I still wanted to make sure I didn't cause extra problems for her.

"Her whereabouts that night was related to her family, but she's afraid if she's honest with the police about it, it'll cause family problems."

"She broke her restraining order?" Aaron guessed.

I nibbled my lip. "You should probably talk to her about this."

"Look, Tabitha, if her ex-husband isn't pressing charges, I have no reason to go after her. I just need to know if anyone can place her in Salem the night of Maple May's murder."

I nodded. "Her ex-husband can. And probably another neighbor, but I'm not sure of the name."

Aaron nodded. "That's enough to go on if we have to confirm her whereabouts after tonight."

While I was at it, I told them both about the Destiny Goddess Statue and how it could be explored as a possible murder weapon if it came to that. "What else did you find out about those blue crystals at the scene of Maple May's death?" I tried to make my voice casual, but I fiddled with Sherlock's tag around his neck, hoping he'd pay attention.

"Not much, unfortunately." This was Jay's department, so he answered. "When questioning the other witches about them, they all tried to pocket them when I wasn't looking, and Marigold even asked if she could buy them from us, once the case was solved."

If that were the case, I suspected Marigold wasn't one of the local witches who had raided my aunt's boat for her sorcery items after her death.

Jay chuckled under his breath and went on. "As if we were ever going to be able to sell evidence."

I thought perhaps he was saying this for Aaron's benefit. Perhaps if it was up to Jay alone, the person who had wanted to purchase my aunt's crystal ball, he may have wanted to find a way to keep the crystals himself.

"I made sure to lock them up extra securely in our evidence lockup, just in case," Aaron put in.

Hmm. That didn't give me much leeway to ask for one, that was for sure.

"I see a light ahead," Jay said. "I'll bet that's the cabin."

It was, but as expected, Frank and his tourists had already vacated it for their

Vision Quest. When we'd pressed Dave more about the nature of a Vision Quest, he seemed to think it was just a matter of taking tourists to remote locations around Crystal Cove where they might sense something in the supernatural. Before we left the office, Dave had shown us Frank's tour website online and how tourists had choices of mountaintop Vision Quests or seaside ones.

As far as he knew, his uncle hadn't truly witnessed any kind of strange phenomenon on any of his tours, but he had lots of stories, as if he had.

"You have the map?" Aaron asked over the seat. "Where do we go from here?"

It was my time to shine. I suddenly got nervous, not wanting to leave the light of the cabin to wander into darkness. But I steeled myself and set the map up on the hood of Jay's car. He shone his phone flashlight so I could see it.

I quickly located the cabin on the map. I'd taken a compass from Frank's office and placed it atop the map to get a handle on which direction we would be headed. It didn't take me long to locate the route Frank should have taken, and then with the help of Jay's flashlight, we found the trailhead.

"This should be it," I said. The trail was wider than I expected, clearly used regularly, with footprints and branches that had been trimmed back.

"Okay, great. Let's go." Aaron's voice was quiet but serious. He led the way. Out here away from the noises of town, it probably wouldn't take much to be heard by other hikers.

Sherlock had followed me out of the car, and when I tried to put him back, he meowed at me and dug his claws in, as if I might not have gotten his point.

So he was coming, too, and now that we were headed into the darkness, I wasn't sure I minded that so much. At the very least, maybe he'd smell any wild animals before they could roam too close.

Jay allowed me to take the middle spot after Aaron and brought up the rear. Soon the trail broke off into two trails, and I had to consult the map again and then pointed Aaron to the left-hand one.

"You're sure you don't have special powers?" Jay asked quietly from behind as we made our way along the trail. "Like Lizzie?"

I shook my head, even though he'd be unlikely to see it. He'd brought a flashlight from his car, too, but had it turned to the lowest setting, so we wouldn't be seen from a distance. "Not me, no," I whispered back. "But I have to admit, on my aunt's boat, I have been experiencing some strange phenomenon." In the dark and quiet, it felt easier to trust someone with this information. Besides, maybe if I told him more, he'd help me find a way to "borrow" another blue crystal to experiment with it.

"What kind of phenomenon?" Aaron said from up front, clearly having heard my quiet voice. He had stopped again at a clearing where several trails broke off. "It seemed like you didn't believe in that sort of thing."

"I didn't," I told him honestly, directing him to the correct path. "But some of it's making me into a believer."

Aaron let out a quiet harrumph.

"What sorts of phenomenon have you seen?" Jay whispered. I had clearly piqued his interest, as his voice took on an excited edge.

"It's hard to put my finger on exactly what." I considered telling him about Sherlock, or about the magically appearing dress, but then Aaron's sudden "Shhh" stopped me.

There were voices in the distance. We'd found them.

Chapter Twenty-eight

FRANK AND HIS TOURISTS were not making any effort to be quiet. In fact, it sounded like they were having fun and joking. Different pitches of laughs came down the trail our way.

Was that his ploy? Bring witches out into the stretches of nowhere, get them off their guard, and then strike them on the back of their heads with an ice ax? And what did he have against witches? Perhaps that was another question we should have asked his nephew.

It would have been difficult to believe this of Frank, but then I'd seen a harder side of him this afternoon, which reminded me I really did not know the man.

The last part of our hike had been on a gentle uphill incline, and now Jay moved ahead of me with his flashlight. The topographical map wasn't necessary when we could follow the sounds of their voices.

It took several long minutes to close in on them, but soon we could follow not only their voices but also the beams of their three flashlights, which were much brighter than Jay's or Aaron's. The detectives turned theirs off.

Sherlock trailed behind us, almost silently, but as we moved within mere feet of the grouping in front of us, he started to purr. Loudly.

Distracted, I stepped on a branch, and it let out a loud crack.

Aaron and Jay both turned back, trying to encourage me and the cat to be quieter. I picked Sherlock up, wondering again if he was trying to give me some sort of hint with the purring.

But just then, one of Frank's tourists asked, "Did you hear that?"

Frank called out, "Is somebody out there?"

Aaron hesitated, but then he turned his flashlight back on. "Frank Markowitz? Is that you?"

"Sure is." Frank's bright flashlight roamed the woods and trail around us. Finally, it landed on Jay. "Who's asking?"

"It's Detective Jameson from the Crystal Cove Police. I just have a few questions, if you could please hold up a minute."

"Sorry, ladies," Frank said to his tourists. "I'm sure this won't take long." Frank made his way back down the trail, nothing but compliant.

He moved closer and came into view under Jay's yellow-y light. Frank became instantly serious when he saw me, along with two police detectives in suits. I gave Sherlock another squeeze, an encouragement to pay attention. He took one look at Frank and let out a long yawn.

That didn't seem right.

"Where are you off to up here tonight?" Aaron asked.

"Just the clearing at the top of this hill, near Alabaster Falls." What Frank said made sense with the topographical map I'd been following. He squinted at me, but before he could ask why I was here, Jay asked the next question.

"And what's your business up there?"

Frank went on to explain the Vision Quest. "Many tourists like to see where our supernatural abundance in Crystal Cove stems from. There are a few thin places near our town, and so I offer tours to let the supernaturally sensitive spend some time in these places to see what they can sense."

I was interested in these "thin places" and wondered if Sherlock would sense anything if I took him right to the clearing where Frank was headed.

But unfortunately, Jay changed tracks before Frank told us anymore. "And can you tell me your whereabouts last Friday night? Were you on one of these tours to these thin places?"

I would have thought Jay would've been the first to believe in something like this, but by his tone, he sounded like a bigger skeptic than I had been.

"Friday? Hmm, let me see." He pulled out his phone and scrolled through it. A flashlight beam waved over us from above. I got the impression his tourists were getting antsy. "Nope, Friday I did a local tour of the town. It was a group of seven tourists."

With his records, the detectives should be able to check that in his file cabinet and perhaps confirm with some of the attendees.

"And what time did this tour run?" Aaron asked. He made notes in his phone, his thumbs flying over the keys.

"It's a tour called Crystal Cove After Dark. It runs from nine until about eleven."

That would provide a solid alibi for Frank if we could confirm it. "Do you have any employees that do tours for you?" I spoke the question as I thought it but felt Aaron's glare and then wanted to slap a hand over my mouth. It wasn't my place to interrogate suspects.

Thankfully, Frank's answer was short and to the point. "Nope. Just me." Now he hit me with an intense glare, too, clearly challenging me for bringing the police after him.

Aaron nodded and slipped his phone away, but there was one more question that occurred to me and I had to ask it. I wanted to check in for Aaron's permission, or even Jay's, but in the dark, I figured I wouldn't get that anyway.

"Was Maple May's tarot card reading on your Crystal Cove After Dark tour?"

Frank bowed his head and nodded. "It was supposed to be. I figured she'd forgotten, like she had a few times in the past." He shook his head. "I was pretty angry with her until I found out what happened."

"Why were you angry?" Aaron pulled out his phone again.

"Two of my tourists asked for refunds because they'd come especially for the tarot readings."

"So you were just angry at her that night?" he confirmed.

Frank nodded. "We had an understanding about promotion, but she could be flighty sometimes, you know?"

"And your understanding . . . did this include going out together?" Jay asked.

Frank looked between me and Jay. "Like I told Tabitha, Maple May was decades too young for me. Maybe some guys are into that sort of thing, but it's not for me. When we met for coffee, it was to discuss promotion. She gave me a kickback for bringing new people in for a Taste of Tarot. Lots of local businesses do that with tour guides. I told Maple May to keep it quiet because I knew how jealous the other witches could get. That's it."

Sherlock purred and let out another yawn, and I felt myself deflate inside. If not Frank, then who had killed Maple May Doerksen?

But thankfully Jay remembered something else I had told him. "What about a secret admirer? Do you know anything about a man that may have been sending Maple May secret gifts?"

Frank shrugged, which I thought meant he didn't know, but then he said, "To me, it seemed pretty obvious it was Avrum from the coffee shop. I mean, every time I met her there, he served her these giant-size drinks with extra whipped cream or pastries he'd made especially for her. Plus, every time I went in there with her, he gave me a major cold shoulder and a lousy drink."

I looked at Jay, and he looked back at me.

"We need to get back," I said, no longer caring if I was overstepping my bounds. "I think Rachael Adams is in trouble!"

Rachael had been planning to get a ride home from Avrum tonight. Not only that, but she planned to pry answers out of him about what he knew about Maple May's secret admirer.

Chapter Twenty-nine

WE GOT BACK TO town, and Jay drove us straight for The Heirloom Café, but we were too late. The closed sign was prominently displayed in the front window.

"I hope she's okay," I murmured more to my cat than to the two detectives.

Jay answered anyway. "Even if he did something to Maple May, chances are good that was personal. It doesn't mean he would hurt Rachael, too."

"But Rachael had planned to bombard him with questions." I groaned and pointed in the direction we should go to get to Rachael's apartment, but Sherlock let out a loud meow.

"Wait." I looked down at the cat, whose gaze was squarely on the front door of the café. "What is it, Sherlock?"

He had his front paws up against my back passenger window.

"Hang on," I told Jay as he was about to pull away. "Maybe there's someone still inside." The more I stared at the café, the more I wondered if I could see flickering candles toward the back upper section.

Aaron sighed. "The place is closed. It's more likely they're headed to her place. We should go."

I was torn. He could be right, and if I kept arguing, they might be too late to get to Rachael in time. But then again, if Sherlock was onto something, and she was still inside . . .

Jay was about to pull away, but I jerked my door open. "Why don't you let me out here? It's only a block to the marina, and I don't want to slow you down."

Jay opened his mouth to say something, but Aaron cut him off with, "Come on, Jameson. If Miss Adams is in danger, we have to get a move on!"

I was out of the car and waving by the time he'd finished his sentence.

Jay watched me in his rearview mirror as he pulled away, but I just continued waving. If Avrum had already taken Rachael home, I wanted them to get to her as soon as possible.

But when Sherlock let out another meow from my arms, now digging his claws in as well, I knew something around here was bothering him.

"Ow!" I whispered and tried to let him down gently, but the cat leaped from my arms. He moved quickly past the front door of the café and around the corner of the brick building that housed it.

I looked both ways down the silent vacant sidewalk and then followed my intuitive cat. I didn't have to move too far around the corner to see where he was headed: the café had a back entrance.

If Sherlock had opposable thumbs, he probably wouldn't need my help. He pawed up at the rear door. I moved in behind him and slowly, silently turned the knob.

It was unlocked.

The back door led to a small walk-in pantry for dried and canned goods. The swinging door in front of us led to the kitchen prep and sales area where Avrum usually stood, and without hesitating, Sherlock headed in that direction.

"Hold on!" I whispered. I still hadn't gotten a handle on what we were doing here or what we might find on the other side of that door.

But it was already too late because Sherlock was through the swinging door.

Only a second later, I realized that while Sherlock might be insightful, leaving him on his own to catch a killer may be putting a little too much faith in the cat.

I got down on my hands and knees and moved an inch at a time through the swinging door, slowly enough that hopefully no one would see the door moving.

As soon as I was halfway through, I heard Rachael's voice. "I just wondered if Frank got that beautiful beaded dreamcatcher from your café here? I know he'd been giving her gifts for a while. If I'd gotten nice gifts like that one, I'd want to know who they were from."

"Well, Markowitz never gave her that," Avrum's voice said. "I put one aside for Maple May when they first came in. I knew she'd love it."

"Oh. Wait. You were her secret admirer?" I couldn't tell by Rachael's tone if this was news to her or if she'd suspected it already. "Well, then you must have met with her on Sunday for her to give you a tarot card reading, right?"

Avrum's voice went suddenly taut. "How did you know about that? Did you tell the police?"

"No, but if you were with her that night . . ." Rachael, unfortunately, wasn't as quick to process this new information as she needed to be.

As her voice became quieter, Avrum cut her off. "You ask too many questions. I always thought you were sweet, but I've learned that appearances can be deceiving. All you witches are the same, taking what you want from others, no matter who it hurts. I'd once thought Maple May was sweet, too. I thought she'd be thrilled to find out I'd been the person sending her gifts, but do you know what she did?" He didn't wait for an answer. "She walked in that night, acting all coy and flirty, then she read my cards, and suddenly she couldn't get out of here fast enough."

"What cards did you get?" Rachael's voice dropped, like she already knew the answer.

He laughed a callous laugh. "It was a picture of a tower. Certainly nothing to freak out about."

"She found out you have shadows and secrets." Rachael's voice was low. Pained. "What did you do to her?"

I could no longer see Sherlock anywhere behind the counter. I scrambled forward, looking for him, and soon realized he must have snuck under the latched half-door to the café. I looked at it, but there was no way I could sneak under it.

"I wouldn't have done anything to her," Avrum said, now almost pleading. "I told her she'd learn I was an okay guy. She'd learn to trust me, but she suddenly wanted nothing to do with me." He went introspective, sounding like he was reassuring himself. "I told her she'd learn to love me back. She just needed time."

"So you did what? You pushed her out into the street and ran over her?" Rachael sounded righteously angry, even if she didn't know all the true details.

I fumbled over my phone and sent three quick numbers and a word to Aaron, as I knew Jay was driving:

911 CAFÉ!

"No! I never would have . . ." Avrum said. "I wanted to take Maple May away with me! But she cast a spell so I wouldn't be able to take her out of Crystal Cove. I thought she was kidding, but when my car suddenly stopped with a screech right at the edge of town, I realized she would ruin my life if I took her back into town. I tried to make her see, tried to hold her back, but she wouldn't stop trying to run back to town. Finally, I grabbed for anything I could find. I knocked her over the head with my pestle, just to slow her down." He shook his head. "I didn't think I'd hit her that hard, but after that, it was too late anyway. Then it was just a matter of saving myself, so I tried to make it look like one of you witches did it."

"How did she cast a spell?" Rachael's voice sounded suddenly strange. Not as worried, more like determined.

"She had some of those blue crystals on a comb in her hair," he said. "She threw it out the car window and yelled out some gobbledygook, and next thing I knew, my car screeched to a stop."

"Blue crystals like this one?" Rachael asked in an ominous voice. It was all I could do not to stand up and look over the counter. Did she really have one? Before I could ask any more internal questions, suddenly Rachael was spouting a mouthful of gobbledygook that sounded something like, "Oshamanda Crocken Anakey!"

I held my breath, and a second later, a crack sounded from the ceiling of the café. I watched in horror as a wooden beam loosened itself and then crashed to the floor.

One second passed. Then two. Then Rachael let out a loud groan in the word, "Noooooooo!"

Avrum chuckled. "It's a good thing you're taking care of fighting yourself off because I had to get rid of my pestle after what happened with Maple May. I couldn't get it clean, and I haven't been able to grind any new spices for almost a week. People are starting to complain." I couldn't believe how detached and calm he sounded, until a second later when his voice held some sudden emotion. "Wait. How did a cat get in here? Get over here, you mangy thing."

I stood to rescue my cat and my new witch friend, but before I could open my mouth and say a word, Aaron moved suddenly through the swinging door behind me.

"Avrum Calloway. Place your hands above your head."

Chapter Thirty

AVRUM'S GAZE DARTED TOWARD Aaron and then to the front door of the café, which was closer to me and to Aaron. Plus, I now saw flashing blue and red lights and a figure on the other side of the glass door, which I suspected was Jay. Avrum took one step in that direction, as if testing his luck, but in one fluid motion, Aaron swept past me and through the half-door, effectively blocking his path.

Reluctant, Avrum froze and did as he was told. I looked to where Aaron had a gun drawn toward him and then to Rachael, who was flat on the floor under a large wooden beam that had to be a foot thick. It pinned her by a shoulder and her opposite hip. By her slow blinks, I suspected she had knocked her head and was losing consciousness.

"Rachael!" I rushed forward, pulling my cell phone to my ear. I had emergency services on the other end by the time I reached Rachael and bent to assess her injuries.

"Stay with me!" I instructed my young witch friend. "We're getting you help. It's going to be okay, Rachael."

Before I'd even given the address of where we were at, Jay had come through the front door and rushed toward us, and Aaron arrested Avrum. Jay took my phone from my hand. He spoke in quiet, quick words and recited several code numbers, which made the 911 call go much quicker than mine had gone the other night.

After he hung up, he helped me lift the beam off Rachael. She shifted and let out a groan, but I was just glad to see her moving.

"Help is on its way." Jay kneeled beside me and checked Rachael's vital signs. Her eyes had closed, but they opened again as Jay touched her neck.

"Detective Jameson?" She looked like she was suddenly pain-free and swept up in a very happy dream.

"Shhh, shhh. Save your strength, Rachael. Help is on the way and you're going to be just fine."

By the sudden bright smile on her face, I didn't doubt it for a minute.

Chapter Thirty-one

IT TOOK A FEW days for Frank to talk to me after the night we'd interrupted his tour up near the cabin. Thankfully, Dave still worked on my aunt's boat every day, but he clammed every time I tried to bring up his uncle.

At first, Frank just claimed busyness, keeping away from the marina most of the days and evenings. But on the third day, I got up early, marched straight up to The Heirloom Café, where I was served by the short-staffed owner, Olivia, and picked up an extra-large star anise brew and a chocolate croissant for him.

Then I sat outside his office until he arrived and passed it over as a peace offering. "I'm really sorry to have insinuated anything about you and Maple May," I told him, now that he was pretty much forced to listen to me. "It was nothing personal. I hope you believe me. It was just a matter of getting to the truth about her death. I'd been the first one on scene, and when I found out it wasn't an accident . . ."

Thankfully, that was all I had to tell him. A couple of sips of his coffee and his mood quickly improved. "I'm sorry, too. That we got off on the wrong foot," he told me.

It was a week later when I finally saw Detective Jay Jameson again. He came walking down the dock with Detective Aaron Thom, both in their suits and wearing happy—or pleasant, in Aaron's case—expressions.

"The Lady of Fortune is back in the water," Jay observed.

"Yes! It's almost done." I smiled up at them from where I sat beside Rachael on the dock. She had been too achy and sore to do her relettering of the boat's moniker while it was dry-docked, but she assured me she'd have no problem painting the letters once it was in the water. She was feeling much better and had already completed "Lady of" this morning.

"That looks great," Jay told Rachael. She blushed hard and waved a hand like it was nothing, but he ignored her embarrassment, or didn't notice it, and added, "You're really talented."

"What's that?" I pointed to a small tin in Jay's hand as I stood, effectively allowing Rachael to regain her breathing.

"I brought a little treat for your feline friend. Is he around?"

"Sherlock?" I called. But I knew exactly where he was. He'd been curled up on the front deck all morning, with one ear perked up, listening to my conversation with Rachael. Apparently, the police had confiscated the blue crystal she'd used at the café a week ago. When being questioned, Rachael had quickly admitted Maple May had given her one to practice with, but that it had been stolen from the Lady of Fortune shortly after Lizzie's death. Aaron had submitted the crystal to the forensics lab for further study, not wanting to release it back to me or my aunt's boat if it was deemed dangerous. I didn't blame him, and now I was more afraid than anxious to have that particular crystal in my possession. I didn't know if it was different from the two Sherlock wore, but I was interested to hear what the forensics department discovered before being in any hurry to take it back.

I'd been plying Rachael with questions about them all morning, and I knew Sherlock would be just as interested.

Sherlock hopped from the deck to the dock, looking wide awake as Jay bent and pried the top off the kitty food can. "You were a big help to us last week."

He still didn't know the details of exactly how Sherlock had helped, but I was thinking of telling him one day soon.

"Did you get Avrum behind bars?" Rachael asked.

Aaron filled in the details of the case. "Not only that, but the Seattle police department told us about an investigation into his dad's death from two years ago when he lived in Seattle. It was deemed an accident at the time, but Avrum was never thoroughly questioned in the matter. I think with these new murder and attempted murder charges, it will give them reason to reopen the case."

I shook my head, barely believing we'd had someone so dangerous living right here in this small town.

"You were instrumental in helping us solve the investigation," Aaron said, and now I felt myself warm. "Thank you."

"Are you getting it up for sale?" Jay motioned to the Lady of Fortune.

"I don't know. I'm suddenly not in such a rush to get back to Portland. I hear the real estate market might need another realtor around Crystal Cove, and in the meantime, the café owner, Olivia, needs a part-time barista. She'll be showing me the ropes tonight during Witchy Wednesday."

I'd been in there every day since Avrum's arrest. Olivia seemed like a nice woman in her late forties. She owned another store in town and was having trouble running both without Avrum's help. I'd quickly offered to step in, at least for now, if I could help.

"I'm glad you're sticking around a little longer." Aaron looked past me, as though he was saying the words to my aunt's boat. "Maybe it'll give us a chance to go for dinner again."

I had the distinct impression that Aaron had invited himself along today to come and see me, and it probably wouldn't have been Jay's first choice. But because Aaron hadn't asked it as a question, I didn't feel obligated to give an outright answer, especially in front of Jay, who was now bent down and talking to Sherlock quietly.

"I haven't had much chance to explore the restaurants in town."

Aaron beamed, taking this as an acceptance of another date. In truth, I wasn't in any hurry to date. My life had turned upside down on me recently, and if I was truly settling in Crystal Cove for the foreseeable future, what I needed most was friends. I hoped Aaron wouldn't take that personally.

He motioned to the boat lettering. "Your aunt would like that. And don't worry, Tabitha. Word travels fast in a small town. Everyone knows she's your aunt, and everyone knows you want to keep that a secret. If you really want people to keep quiet about it, you'd be best to just be honest. People in small towns don't want to start a big political scandal. They just want to know who everyone is."

The idea of people knowing who I— and my family—was brought a mix of fear and relief. Maybe he was right, though. Trying to keep secrets in a small town may not be the best way forward if I was planning to stay for any length of time, and wasn't it time I figured out who I really was?

"What do you know about things going on under the surface, huh?" Jay asked my cat. I'd been thinking of Sherlock more and more as my cat. If I was staying in town, there seemed like no immediate reason to look for a new home for him. Although, if I needed one, with the way Jay was fawning over my little feline friend, I didn't doubt he'd be quick to adopt him. He reached for Sherlock's tag with the embedded blue crystal, and Sherlock was too busy eating his little treat to notice.

Before Jay could get a good look at it, I snatched the cat up in my arms. Jay looked from Sherlock's glasses to his tag and back again. When he looked up at me, he opened his mouth to ask something, but I gave my head a minuscule shake.

Thankfully, he took the hint.

But then he said, "Maybe I'll have to take you for dinner sometime soon, too." Aaron's gaze snapped to Jay and so did Rachael's. He quickly added. "You know, to introduce you to some of the local restaurants."

Great, had I somehow worked my way in between these two local detectives, not to mention made my best witch friend in town jealous?

I would need to tell them both—and soon—that I wasn't interested in a relationship.

Thankfully, they soon left, again both telling me how happy they were that I was sticking around Crystal Cove. I was happy, too, except for the matter of phoning my dad to let him know about my decision.

I didn't expect him to understand that this was the first time in my life that I'd felt useful and like I belonged somewhere. I expected to hear an earful.

But it was time to start standing up to him, rather than using all my energy worrying what the senator thought about me and my choices. They were my choices, after all.

Crystal Cove made me feel like I could make good decisions all on my own for the first time in my life.

"What do you think?" Rachael asked. She stood back at a distance to look over her workmanship.

It felt like a relief that my aunt's boat was back to being the Lady of Fortune.

And I wasn't sure how, but somehow I knew I belonged here aboard this boat, just as much as she had.

I'd be the new Lady of Fortune. It was time to figure out where my own fortune lay.

THE END

Up Next: Thrilling Thursday

TABBY IS SETTLING INTO Crystal Cove and her new home on a magic-infused houseboat when the summer fair comes to town. She and her newly inherited cat, Sherlock, man the coffee truck while screams of excitement erupt from the nearby rides. Soon the fun screams turn to shrieks of horror when a dead body is discovered on one of the rides, and Tabby may be the only one who can help her detective friends figure out how it got there.

Apparently, Crystal Cove has no shortage of secrets or murders, and once again, Tabby may be the only person who can see through its shroud of illusions.

Order Thrilling Thursday now to continue reading!

Reviews Matter...

HONEST REVIEWS HELP BRING new books to the attention of other readers. If you enjoyed this book, I would be grateful if you would take five minutes to write a couple of sentences about it.

You can find it at this link: https://books2read.com/witchywednes day

Thank you so much for your support. I couldn't do this without readers like you!

Join My Cozy Mystery Readers' Newsletter Today!

Would you like to be among the first to hear about new releases and sales, and receive special excerpts and behind-the-scene bonuses?

Sign up now to get your free copy of **Mystery of the Holiday Hustle – A Mallory Beck Cozy Holiday Mystery**.

You'll also get access to special epilogues to accompany this series—an exclusive bonus for newsletter subscribers. Sign up below and receive your free mystery: https://www.subscribepage.com/mysteryreaders

Recipe: The Heirloom Café's Lavender Latte

NOTHING BEATS A TASTE and unique latte to make you feel cozy inside! Whip up a batch of this lavender simple syrup and you'll be ready for a special latte at a moment's notice.

Lavender Simple Syrup Ingredients:

¼ cup dried lavender

½ cup water

½ cup white sugar

Instructions:

Add water and lavender to a small saucepan and bring to a boil. Reduce heat and simmer for 2-3 minutes. Remove from heat and let cool completely.

Use a mesh strainer to separate the buds from the water.

In another saucepan combine the sugar with 2-3 tablespoons of the lavender water (just enough to wet the sugar). Bring to a boil, reduce heat and let simmer for 4 minutes. Whisk occasionally.

Whisk the lavender water into the sugar mixture and store in the refrigerator.

Lavender Latte Ingredients:
½ cup milk (I used whole)
⅔ cup strong brewed coffee
2 Tablespoons Lavender simple syrup (more or less to personal liking)

Instructions:
Brew coffee and pour into your desired mug. Add simple syrup and stir.

Warm your milk on the stove and then froth with a milk frother or pour the milk into any kind of blender and blend for 30 seconds.

Pour milk over top of coffee and syrup mixture and sprinkle with dried lavender. Enjoy!

Recipe: Nutmeg Brown Sugar Coffee Cake

THIS SPICED COFFEE CAKE will make the perfect accompaniment to your lavender latte.

Ingredients

2 cups dark brown sugar, firmly packed

2 cups baking flour, sifted

1 teaspoon baking powder

1 pinch salt

½ cup cold butter, roughly chopped

1 teaspoon baking soda

1 cup milk

1 egg, lightly beaten

1 teaspoon ground nutmeg

1/2 cup pecans, chopped

ground cinnamon (to taste)

Directions

Preheat oven to 350 degrees F.

Grease a 9 inch square pan, and line with baking paper.

Combine flour, baking powder and salt, then rub in the butter until the mixture resembles fine breadcrumbs.

Then add sugar, and combine.

Press half this mixture evenly over the base of the prepared cake pan, and reserve other half.

Dissolve baking soda in milk, add beaten egg and nutmeg, then add to reserved mixture.

Combine well.

Pour into the pan and sprinkle nuts, and cinnamon over top.

Bake in oven for 45 minutes to 60 minutes (start testing for doneness with a skewer after about 45 minutes).

Allow to stand for 10 minutes before turning onto a wire rack to cool.

Enjoy!

Acknowledgements

Thank you to my amazing team of advance readers, brainstormers, and supporters. I am so very thankful for every single one of you!
Thank you to my developmental editor, Louise Bates, my copyeditor, Sara Burgess, and my "Strange Facts Expert" Danielle Lucas. My books would not be nearly as good without you!
Thank you for joining me, along with Tabby and Sherlock, on this journey. We're thrilled to have you along on this ride!

<u>**THE TABITHA CHASE DAYS of the Week Mysteries**</u>

Book 1 - Witchy Wednesday
Book 2 - Thrilling Thursday
More titles coming soon!

<u>**The Mallory Beck Cozy Culinary Capers:**</u>

Book 1 – Murder at Mile Marker 18
Book 2 – Murder at the Church Picnic
Book 3 – Murder at the Town Hall
Christmas Novella – Mystery of the Holiday Hustle
Book 4 – Murder in the Vineyard
Book 5 – Murder in the Montrose Mansion
Book 6 – Murder during the Antique Auction
Book 7 – Murder in the Secret Cold Case
Book 8 – Murder in New Orleans
Find all the Mallory Beck novels at bit.ly/MalloryBeck!

<u>**Collaborative Works:**</u>

Murder on the Boardwalk
Murder on Location
Saving Heart & Home

<u>**Nonfiction for Writers:**</u>

Writing with a Heavy Heart
Story Sparks
Fast Fiction

Denise Jaden is a co-author of the Rosa Reed Mystery Series by Lee Strauss, the author of several critically-acclaimed young adult novels, as well as the author of a few nonfiction books for writers, including the NaNoWriMo-popular guide Fast Fiction.

Her cozy mystery series', The Mallory Beck Cozy Culinary Capers and The Tabitha Chase Days of the Week Mysteries will continue to launch throughout this year. In her spare time, she acts in TV and movies and dances with a Polynesian dance troupe. She lives just outside Vancouver, British Columbia, with her husband, son, and one very spoiled cat.

Sign up on Denise's website to receive bonus content as well as updates on her new Cozy Mystery Series.

www.denisejaden.com